JAMBOREE

Michael Upchurch

JAMBOREE

Alfred A. Knopf · New York · 1981

This is a Borzoi Book
Published by Alfred A. Knopf, Inc.

Copyright © 1981 by Michael Upchurch
All rights reserved under International and
Pan-American Copyright Conventions.
Published in the United States by Alfred A.
Knopf, Inc., New York, and simultaneously
in Canada by Random House of Canada
Limited, Toronto. Distributed by Random
House, Inc., New York.

Library of Congress
Cataloging in Publication Data
Upchurch, Michael, [date]
Jamboree
I. Title
PS3571.P375J3   813'.54   80-18489
ISBN 0-394-51150-6

Manufactured in the
United States of America
First Edition

With deep thanks, to Maxine

JAMBOREE

"Hangman's noose," Mr. Berringer said, and held it up for the boys in the back seat to see; the noose swayed a little, back and forth, in light which came through the windshield.

United States Boy Scout Troop 431 was on its way to a mini-jamboree of the Northwest New Jersey Council, on Sandy Hook. Three troop leaders, two assisting fathers, and a number of mothers with boys, leaning close or keeping their distance, had all met in the Presbyterian church parking lot at seven o'clock that morning. Mr. Berringer had gotten there first in his pickup truck with his wife and two boys, Clay and Blue, arriving half an hour early, at six-thirty, in the event that others might do so too and allow them to get an even earlier start than the troop as a whole had envisaged. This had seemed not at all an unlikely possibility to the Berringers, the only family connected with the troop who were in the regular habit of getting up at five o'clock in the morning, at which time of day they did all their chores—Mr. Berringer tidied up his shop (he was a carpenter), Mrs. Berringer did her housework, and the boys did their homework. Getting up at five in the morning was nothing they were overly proud of or ever tried to make other people do, however, and when, on the last camping trip, the Bray twins had struggled out of their tent at eight o'clock on a midsummer morning and seen the sun at less than a forty-five-degree angle in the sky to the east, prompting Roger Bray to start dancing and pointing and shouting: "Dawn! Hey! Look—it's dawn!," Clay and Blue Berringer hadn't said a word but only stared in the direction that was being pointed out to them as though the morning sun astonished them as much as it did Roger. Dawn, which along with dusk was their favorite time of day, didn't seem a thing to get excited over or boast about, but only something to discover. In an entirely unspoken way, they both felt they had their father to thank for arranging their discovery of it, and the fact that a Bray twin should mistake mid-morning for dawn did not surprise them at all because they both, again in an unspoken way, did not see how anyone who had Mr. Bray for a father would ever be likely to discover anything.

While the sun rose and began to cast long shadows and bright slivers of light through trees and shrubbery and across suburban lawns, the Berringers sat—Clay and Blue and Mr. Berringer occupying one half of the cab in the front of the truck while Mrs. Berringer filled the other, the two boys and their father being wiry and slim, while Mrs. Berringer was enormous and fat. Mr. Berringer had let the motor idle for a short while after they'd gotten there, thinking that they might immediately be joined by the others and hit the road, but when it became apparent that this would not be the case, he shut the motor off and they fell into silence, staring out the windshield at the empty church parking lot. Light from around them faintly lit their faces green and made them look like visitors from another planet, established and settled in their ways, almost ascetic, and unable to take advantage of the comforts and convenience which surrounded them, into which they had either driven or been driven or had stumbled, they could hardly say.

They waited.

After ten minutes, at a quarter to seven, the Davieses arrived in their little sports car, with Mrs. Davies driving, Mr. Davies in the passenger seat, and Chris Castle, Mrs. Davies's son, curled up in the back. Mr. Davies, out of a habit of leaving a reliable margin of time to ensure making connections between plane and train and airport limousine (he worked for an international electronics corporation and made frequent business trips), always arrived at his appointments and points of departure fifteen minutes early, often with both his wife and stepson on hand in the event of any unforeseen complication. Laura Davies pulled around so that their car faced the pickup truck and then she peered up and, through the windshield, smiled and waved at the Berringers. Mrs. Berringer smiled and waved back doubtfully, as though uncertain what Laura Davies's smile could portend, while Mr. Berringer opened the door of his cab and hopped down.

Ian Davies got out of his car too and Chris followed suit, to stretch his legs, only he didn't tag along with his stepfather.

Mr. Davies and Mr. Berringer approached each other, shook hands, and, simultaneously, made the same comment:

"Nobody here yet."

"Anybody here yet?"

Then they stood in silence and looked around. The present peace of the scene seemed a haven and a respite, in anticipation of the noise and scheduled events to come. Both cars were shut off and quiet like ghosts. Laura Davies and Mrs. Berringer had dropped their eyes back down to their laps, Mrs. Berringer to return to her knitting, Laura to browse through a copy of *Forbes* business magazine. The Berringer boys had both gotten out and were walking around, but they didn't go near Chris Castle or the two men.

Then, at about a quarter past seven, more cars started to come in. Younger boys in uniform were dropped off by mothers or fathers to accumulate in a crowd out of which their faces stared, half in excitement, half in fear. Mr. Wing, one of the assistant scoutmasters, came in a station wagon loaded with his three sons and all kinds of camping equipment to be distributed among his and Mr. Gough's cars and Mr. Berringer's truck. He took charge of the boys, walked round and round the outskirts of the crowd—and just his presence, with his shock of stiff red hair sticking straight up and his high clear voice, were reassuring and, moreover, a much better way to start the day than with the real scoutmaster, Mr. Gough. Their comfort and reassurance with Mr. Wing were short-lived, however, because in a few minutes—at exactly the same time that Mr. Bray, the other assistant scoutmaster, and his twins arrived in their Toyota driven by Mrs. Bray, who was still in her gauzy pink nightgown and quilted polyester bathrobe but wide awake and cheery now that she was out of the house and in company —the Gough entourage arrived too, with Mr. Gough and his son, Jim (who would turn sixteen next month), in the station wagon and Mrs. Gough and Jim's older sister, Mindy, following behind in the Volkswagen. This put everything in full swing, leaving everyone uncertain as to what would happen next.

Cars were parked all askew, the Davieses and the Berringers having given no one any firm idea of a pattern to be followed. Mr. Gough heaved his bulk between car fenders, trying to follow up on arrangements and get some sense out of Mr. Wing, who was ranging around, at large, asking the question "Is everybody happy?"—to which some boys answered in chorus yes while other boys answered nothing at all. Mr. Bray got out of his car and followed Mr. Gough with his eyes, while the twins shot past him and danced around, trying to attract the attention of Jim Gough, who, at this point, in the presence of his father, made no response. The Bray twins didn't care if their father was there or not, because their mother was and so was Mindy Gough, and that meant that as long as they didn't make a mess, which they couldn't do because they weren't in a house, they could do anything they wanted.

Mrs. Gough got out of the Volkswagen and tried to look out for things to tell people to do and mistakes her husband might make, but Mindy stayed in the passenger seat, smiling at her little brother and thinking of what she could do with him. His scout hat, she noticed, was folded and tucked neatly into his belt. In order to remedy this and take her opportunity she caught his eye, and then she mouthed at him with an air that referred to a longstanding habit between them, "Put on your hat, put on your hat." She liked to see him dressed up, she liked to see him slowly put on his full uniform a piece at a time—and then, just as slowly, piece by piece, take the uniform off. He usually didn't mind complying. But just now, as with the twins, he didn't pay attention to her.

He was the oldest of the boys in this troop and he was the troop leader even though he was only a Life scout, and Blue Berringer would soon be an Eagle. This past summer had made a change; it had been months since he had taken part in any scout project with his father with any kind of enthusiasm. More to the point, his taste had died for taking any pleasure in forcing boys younger than himself to do something they didn't want to do. He'd become detached in the midst of them, unable to take an interest in anyone connected with the troop except the Bray twins, and that, to the younger boys, had succeeded in making him a more frightening and ominous figure than, during all the year before, a consistent policy of persecution had done. He was just becoming aware of his role as other people's plaything — a kind of sounding board for his mother and father's conflicting claims to power and ascendancy within their marriage and a sounding board of another kind for his sister, although the pleasures connected with this latter role were too delectable to give up simply to overcome a feeling of being used.

One result of this growing awareness had been a new distaste for exercising control over other people. Since all contacts seemed to be either an exercising of power or a falling within the scope of someone else's power, Jim had pulled back from most contacts on either side, as he thought of it, and now held an untenable, slightly floating, tense position, from which it felt as if there were nowhere to go. His sister was smiling at him and mouthing words, telling him what she wanted him to do—for her to see him in full uniform right here in the parking lot in front of everyone else was as arousing as it was to see him in private piece by piece take the uniform off—but he pretended to ignore her, looking instead at the trees or at Chris Castle's mother, who was different, somehow, from all the other mothers of the boys in the troop, not so friendly or foolish. She sat by herself in her car and her husband and Chris stood outside, looking at the scene in general, not saying a word.

This led Jim to think that, although he harbored a dislike of Mr. Davies and his stepson (it was, perhaps, a class resentment as much as anything else—the Goughs lived in a very different part of town from the Davieses and, rather than working for a big corporation, Mr. Gough was a phys. ed. teacher in a high school in a neighboring township while Mrs. Gough worked in the ticket booth of a local movie theater), he might have more in common with those two than he had previously been willing to admit, seeing as how he and Mr. Davies and Chris were all at this moment doing more or less the exact same thing—standing in a parking lot, saying nothing to anybody, and appearing to have no plans or intentions to do so.

Things were happening to him, though, that weren't happening to either of them; claims were being made. Mindy was smiling out the car window at him and at the Bray twins, and his ignoring her was making the Bray twins giggle and clutch each other and even shriek. This was like a laughter out of nowhere, which made so little sense that it finally forced Jim to smile and turn and try to figure out what was going on by looking at his sister: who turned her face away then, looked at the dashboard, and smiled deep, very deep, to herself. Jim couldn't win, he couldn't figure out what order the Brays' laughter, Mindy's smile, and his own reluctance to obey or take an interest were coming in; and as if to put a lid on any figuring out of any order, a chorus of voices drowned his thoughts out with an order of their own.

It was Mr. Wing leading the younger boys of the troop in a rousing rendition of "If You're Happy and You Know

It Clap Your Hands," while Jim's father, Mr. Gough, glared and muttered and Mr. Bray stared dully, having a headache. Mrs. Bray, bright and cheerful, was clapping along, however, while Mr. Berringer and his two boys ignored the ruckus and loaded all sorts of camping items into the back of the truck. Mrs. Berringer sat in the cab like an enormous mountain of flesh that someone had left behind, looking up from her knitting occasionally with a slightly quizzical look on her face as if surprised by the moment and the remembering of where she was. It was at one of these moments that Mrs. Gough, chain smoking and looking grim, stalking along with her hair still in curlers, found what was wrong and made her accusation. She pointed a finger straight at Mrs. Berringer. And at first Mrs. Berringer hadn't known what Mrs. Gough meant by it—it seemed to her that she was only a little more on the heavy side than Mrs. Gough, her own inordinate size being the first thing she thought of, though she kept this to herself, in any contact with another woman. But Mrs. Gough soon made her point clear: Mr. Berringer's pickup truck had come under her consideration and been diagnosed; and her diagnosis proclaimed it to be unsafe. What if one of the Bray twins were to climb up onto the roof of the cab and jump off? They'd both broken arms, their own and others', the last few times they'd gone camping.

Everything had to come to a halt and then start over. Clay and Blue had to climb up into the back of their father's pickup truck and throw equipment down to be packed into Mr. Wing's station wagon again. Mr. Gough's station wagon was also packed with more equipment than had previously been envisaged. A consensus was taken and it was agreed that Mr. Bray's Toyota would have to be expropriated from his wife, which left Mrs. Bray standing in the parking lot in her bathrobe, no longer clapping, wondering aloud what was going to happen to her—whereupon it was arranged that Mrs. Berringer would give Mrs. Bray a lift home in the now obsolete truck. Mr. Bray and Mr. Berringer were inserted into the front seat of the Toyota with three pup tents piled between them, while a Bray twin, Billy, and the youngest Wing, Anthony, and Chuckie Massie were put in the back, with backpacks and mildewed cooking equipment piled in their laps and at their feet. Mr. Wing, meanwhile, was the chauffeur, as planned, of the two Berringers, Danny McDaniels, and two of the younger boys, taking along Jim Gough to help supervise them. And Jim's father, Mr. James Gough, Senior, in his full scoutmaster uniform and with an old military cap now perched on his crewcut head, was to transport the remaining Bray twin, the two oldest Wings, Mr. Davies, and Chris Castle. All the shuffling and reconsideration and redistribution took much longer than anticipated, Mrs. Gough did not really look any happier with the arrangement as it eventually emerged than she'd been with it before she'd tried her hand, and the convoy did not really get underway and exeunt from the lovely suburbs until what was called, by a tacit agreement among the three scoutmasters involved, eight o'clock—"Well, eight o'clock isn't bad!"—but was in fact closer, according to the hands on the church steeple shining tall and gold-plated in the now brightening morning, to twenty past.

Mr. Gough led the way, the other two cars followed, through sleepy streets, along familiar thoroughfares in the pretty town of Waynesboro in Somerset County. They passed through the town center with its renovated shop fronts and boutiques, they passed through developments, with their row upon row of "colonial" houses, and then they got onto the highway which passed along the edge of town.

"On the road!" Mr. Wing, who still was young, declared and stepped on the accelerator to pull up parallel with Mr. Gough, Senior, so that the boys in the two cars could wave to each other, while Jim Gough hung low, looked out a window at neutral margins of ragweed, goldenrod, dandelions, and crabgrass which grew from the edge of the highway to the edges of neatly manicured and bleak suburban lawns. Boys spotted houses where they, or friends of theirs or girls who they talked about, lived. Tired Mr. Bray fell farther and farther behind in his car, where he and Mr. Berringer didn't say a word to each other. And then the convoy was out of town, traveling over the crest of a wooded hill, where the highway cut an edge through blasted rock—a spur of the Watchungs.

They picked up 287 south, and came from behind a barrier of hills. Excitement intensified. They traveled through a no-man's-land of flat fields and industrial parks, scattered residential areas with houses which looked somehow much more cramped and oppressed than the ones in which these boys from Waynesboro lived. Sun shone down on the Watchungs. It was the first cool day of autumn. Air from Canada had pressured off the heavy-laden sultry air of August (this was Labor Day weekend) and made a cool start for September. Leaves were just beginning to turn color here and there. The Watchungs were like a man's long resting arm which, as if by a sleeve, was covered in a layer of leaves; their ridge came three or four hundred feet up from the plain and stayed a reference point as the convoy trailed away.

Mr. Wing was the only one of the drivers who let his boys listen to the radio. Jim Gough fiddled with the

dial, found and turned up Harry Harrison on WABC—
who was playing Stevie Wonder doing "You Are the
Sunshine of My Life." The song rang out over the cars'
highway whine, the freight trucks' roar. Mr. Wing winced,
said: "Not so loud." He leaned to adjust the volume,
then turned to Jim and smiled. Jim Gough looked back
at him and neither smiled nor looked unfriendly, but
only said, "Mr. Bray's gonna get lost, if he can't keep up
with us—got lost last time." Then he turned his glance
toward an increasingly meaningless landscape, a jumble
of landscapes—billboards, clover leaves, power stations.
He stole an occasional look at Mr. Wing. Mr. Wing held
his head up high, looked down the highway, and had a
constant smile on his face as though each bend in the
road were an old friend to him, a cause for celebration;
as though the vision of a face informed the sunlight
which came crisp and clear now from above.

Mr. Wing was thirty-four years old. He had three
sons, Mark, Michael, and Anthony, who were thirteen,
twelve, and eleven years old respectively. He was of Irish
descent and his voice had a soft lilt to it although he had
never been to the country where his father and his grandparents had all been born. He had frizzy red hair, which
he had been losing lately, so that his forehead had gotten
higher and higher, more and more optimistic as it went
—and he had a trimmed but flaring mustache. His blue
eyes were like a morning light at sea and conveyed an
absolute confidence, a quiet but insurmountable nervous
energy. Mark, Michael, and Anthony were carbon copies
of him, all like small Mr. Wings, only without the
mustache, and with ways and quiet pleasures of their
own, secrets one could hardly name but whose presence
was unmistakable, with a trait that was more easily
detected in the boys than in their father—a shyness,

amounting almost to a terror sometimes, in their dealings with the outside world. The periodic appearance of Mrs. Wing at scout functions gave no clue—when with her, Mr. Wing's happiness appeared to soar and she in turn became a mere extension of his radiance, no contrast, until with their arms around each other, smiling (they were always embarrassingly affectionate together in public), they made a kind of unreal sky, beneath which their boys were secretly free. For all one knew, he might have invented his own name.

Jim Gough looked at him again, and thought of the three Wings, so much alike and so close together in age as to make Mr. Wing seem a champion of sex of the most potent variety—and yet there was no one more like a chipmunk, less like a cad, than Mr. Wing. No one of the adults (Jim Gough was losing interest in the boys; only the Bray twins had proved themselves worthy of his patronage) was more pleasant and less comprehensible to be with than Mr. Wing. But the incomprehensibility was wearing thin with Jim just now. . . .

"If Mr. Bray gets lost," Mr. Wing replied, with no sarcastic intent, "he'll eventually find us," and drove on.

The two Berringers, Danny McDaniels, and the smaller boys looked on at the two grown men (for the age difference between Jim Gough and Mr. Wing seemed, at least to the younger boys, negligible) in awe and silence, interrupted only by occasional whispering when they were distracted by things outside—"Look . . . a boat," Danny pointing to a barge of some sort as they crossed the lower Raritan. But the greater part of their attention was held by and they understood, in all but words, the terrible gap between Jim Gough and Mr. Wing, each boy fearing what the one might do to the other, each boy secretly relieved that they had apparently decided

to have nothing to do with each other, having slipped
into an abeyant rather than a tense détente.

Mr. Wing's eyes concentrated on the road. His mind
kept on his task of driving (when Mr. Wing took on a
responsibility such as the safe and orderly conduct from
Waynesboro to Sandy Hook in his car of six boys with
whose lives and moral well-being he felt himself to be
entrusted, he held on to the task deliberately, consciously,
and conscientiously, as onto some difficult prism which
he must learn to balance and not let shatter) while Jim
Gough kept his eyes out the window, off the road (on
grill joints and bars housed in converted streetcars or
railway carriages, on retail outlets made of concrete and
plastic and glass set adrift in seas of asphalt that spread
out from highway entrances and exits, on sad houses
too close to the highway in which Blacks lived, sitting
on their porches, watching cars go by) as though it were
some equally important task he was performing by
looking outside. Had it been Mrs. Wing, instead of Jim,
at Mr. Wing's side, she would (they knew) have twisted
around in the front seat, always addressing them, giving
them unnecessary things to eat, Cheez Doodles and
pretzels, and telling them about the things that little
boys might be thinking about on a journey such as this
(she would be wrong—they were all of them thinking,
when their minds weren't on the contrast between Mr.
Wing and Jim Gough immediately before them, about
Jim's older sister, Mindy), only occasionally diverting
the flow of this monologue from the boys in the back to
her husband in the front, whom she would have addressed
as though he were the youngest boy of them all as he
held his mouth open for her to insert pretzels and
whatever-else into it, without his ever taking his eyes off
the road, the prism held firm, in a life that was (Mrs.

Wing looked just like a little girl, with that purple chiffon scarf tied in her soft blond hair) as perfect in its balance as could be.

But it was not Mrs. Wing in the car with them, it was Jim Gough, and that made them all (even Mr. Wing) think, for a brief moment, and then repulse the thought (Mr. Wing lost all confidence in his presence) of Jim's father, Mr. Gough, who had sped right out of sight in the car ahead.

The two leading cars, a mile apart, with Mr. Bray lagging unknown miles behind them, had crossed the New Jersey Turnpike and were on the Garden State Parkway now, traveling through the last stretch of an industrial landscape, with its feeling of pollution and cattails and stagnant waters all around. Ahead of them, there began to be trees once more and small hills and a string of small towns.

Mr. Gough had, the minute he'd pulled onto 287, peremptorily ordered, "Roll your windows up." The boys in back rolled theirs up immediately, but Mr. Davies had simply looked at Mr. Gough in surprise and incomprehension.

Mr. Gough, unfazed by this reaction, elaborated on his order: "Roll your windows up and I'll put on the air conditioner."

Mr. Davies rolled up his window slowly—it could not possibly have been more than sixty-five degrees outside and, although it might warm up later on, just now he could not see any need for an air conditioner at all.

But Mr. Gough could not have been more pleased. With all the windows rolled up, he leaned over (his military cap would not stay on his head) and adjusted certain levers on his dashboard, which made a fatigued whining and whirring noise and then proceeded to release jets of chilly, iron-smelling air onto Mr. Davies's chest and knees, while the back of the station wagon began to grow stuffy. This accomplished, Mr. Gough turned to his fellow passenger and asked in a gruff but pleasant tone, "You never been down here before?"

Mr. Davies had to admit that he hadn't.

"Well, you're gonna like it," Mr. Gough insisted. "It's an *ideel* place, it's an *ideel* location, it's just sand goin' out into the ocean. I guess you got nothin' like it in England?" he asked Mr. Davies, who was English.

Mr. Davies said that, well, actually there was a rather famous beach made of shingle, called the Chesil Beach, about twenty miles long, he thought, on the south coast, near Weymouth; he'd had friends at university who were geologists who'd said it was the largest of its kind in the world—

"Well, you're gonna like this then, you're gonna get a kick outa this," Mr. Gough said (Mr. Davies could not have given a better answer), then turned around and bellowed into the back seat, "Cut the goddamn hell out!" to boys who were acting up (Roger Bray was trying to stir up the two Wings, Mark and Michael, with a fair amount of success, by doing an imitation of Mindy Gough acting sexy), then turned back to Mr. Davies, looked important, and added, " 'Cause I'm in the reserves there."

Mr. Davies didn't follow. "In the reserves where?"

"On Sandy Hook."

"Oh—do the military use the parks? I didn't think they did that here."

"No, no, they got it divided in two—half park, half military. They got a little base right at the top of the Hook."

They drove on in silence for a minute, Roger Bray and the two Wings quiet now, repressed. Mr. Davies's son

Chris, looked out the window of the car, then looked at Mr. Gough. Mr. Gough was well worth watching—he had a thought or a question rising in him, and it was as painful to watch as any strenuous, demanding animal rhythm (the giving of birth, the difficult emptying of bowels); the thought was like a sticky, messy substance trying to struggle out of the pit of Mr. Gough's brain up into and around his puglike face and squinched eyes, till it finally came out half through his mouth, half through his nose—

"You mean the military got use of all the *parks* in England?"

"Well, if you aren't careful on Dartmoor," Mr. Davies said, getting his first real pleasure out of the conversation, "you're liable to get your head blown off."

"No kiddin'—they shoot civilians?"

"Well, they try not to, they try to be careful."

"And they use the parks?"

"Actually, I don't think I've ever heard of a civilian getting shot. They just have a lot of signs up all around telling you not to go any farther."

"Oh."

And then there was silence again. Mr. Gough had to concentrate. He had to make sure he got the right exit off the parkway, which he nearly always missed. The parkway turned south, while the road he wanted kept going east to the Jersey shore, with Raritan Bay on one side and a low-lying hill on the other. Chris Castle was sitting on the hill side of the car. There were houses on the hill that had a different look from the houses in Waynesboro. They were older and they looked out over more of an expanse. They weren't beach houses, but something more durably built and yet open to the light; they seemed, many of them, to have glass verandas around them and sunrooms, cupolas at their tops, which would make even the coming winter seem a season one could look out into, not hide away from, and see how it affected the land sloping down, the bay below and the sky above, and the big city across the bay, too, which you could perhaps see, see its skyline, on a day clearer than this one.

Chris tried looking across the back seat of the car out to the water, which the road came within a few hundred yards of sometimes, but the view was always partially blocked by the head of someone or by a house or a tree or by telephone and electric wires, and even when he got a glimpse it wasn't satisfying in the way it should be, it had none of that freedom or reach which the word "bay" conjures up. It was white and had no beach, but only a shoreline, trailing off in cattails which looked as though they might be dirty. As the cars approached the edge of land, a smog or sea haze started to surround them, so that even when they were on a rise the bay had no definite outline, and after craning and twisting for five minutes or more to see one, Chris finally gave it up and decided to settle for the houses on the hill to the right again—only to find that now the hill had gotten so close that he couldn't see those either. He turned to look back at the two cars which were supposed to be following, but they were both out of sight, Mr. Wing most likely keeping within the speed limit and staying steadily a mile or two behind them (they were almost there and the difference in the vegetation and the houses and the feel of things began to make Roger Bray and the two Wings restless) while Mr. Bray was probably hopelessly lost with only Mr. Berringer—who could find his own way easily enough, but could never give directions— to help him in and out of the plethora of highway exits and entrances that riddled the no-man's-land beyond Perth Amboy.

Chris sat up straight in the back seat then and looked ahead. He didn't have much to do with the other boys, partly because he had moved to Waynesboro in the middle of a school year and he knew from past experience, in moving from the United States to England four years earlier, that there was no point in trying to make friends with anyone until a new school year began (as it would in a week) and the reshuffling of old classes and new arrivals broke up established cliques. But he also kept to himself, in part, because he was quiet and didn't care, he was used to entertaining himself, and, unlike most of the other boys in this troop, he was used to talking to grownups. At least, he talked in a direct and intelligent way with his mother and with his stepfather, Ian; but he was beginning for the first time to have some doubts as to his ability to talk with grownups in general after having come across the same trouble he had in talking with boys his own age whenever he had to try to make contact with Mr. Gough (here, he toyed with the possible explanation that Mr. Gough had not yet taken the vital step up the evolutionary ladder from Neanderthal man, and so didn't know how to talk) or Mr. Wing (whose nuptial bliss was too much to take) or Mr. Bray (although not so much because of any particular character trait of Mr. Bray's as because of the fact that Mr. Bray seemed always too tired to talk or to distinguish one boy from another). Mr. Bray was the only one, Chris knew, whom Ian could talk to (even if it was only just a little bit), although of course there was Mr. Berringer, who was wily and vigorous and old and whom everyone was able to listen to much as they might read a yellowing book. All in all, the people who surrounded him, both those his own age and those his parents had come in touch with and invited over for a drink, had seemed incomprehensible for the past nine months, imbued with a foreignness which would not dispel or come clearer.

He recognized well enough that he, after three years in an English school, and his stepfather, by birth, were the true foreigners in this situation; and he knew also, from having moved before, that parts of himself, with a little time, would eventually disappear, allowing him to seem to be more a part of the thing he was surrounded by. But the process seemed to be particularly slow in Waynesboro—it seemed not even to have begun. When, after all, would these people ever reveal themselves, having through motions of friendliness and openness and assumption and intrusion so effectively hidden themselves at the outset—or were they really as simple as they made out they were? And, if this was so, what was the point in staying here and what did these people, Mr. Gough, Mr. Wing, Mr. Bray, Mr. Berringer, think their lives could mean that they made so little perceptible reference to them? It was a lack of reference and a lack of meaning that had begun unconsciously to trouble Chris and make him not want to go (there seemed no point) outside his small family circle, not want physically to leave the "colonial" house which fitted the three of them, a house where habits, assumptions, and trains of thought were followed which had no outward corresponding manifestation in Waynesboro that he could detect or that he could read, however tenuously, into things which could not help but capture his attention—unabashed public laughter here, and equally shameless public tears there, moments of real exposure which gave no clue, gave away nothing. Nor did his classmates' strange absorption and mimickry of idiotic television commercials give any clue.

But he was not the kind of child to grow dismayed at living with things which were, for the moment, beyond his comprehension—his reaction was to simply stay cool, watchful.

They had lived in Waynesboro for nine months now; they might easily stay on another nine. Ian's project gave no sign, that Chris could detect, of being about to draw to a close.

But the thought of even the possibility of a move drew Chris's attention to his stepfather, sitting in the front passenger seat, apparently staring out the front windshield, so that all Chris could see was the back of his head.

Ian Davies, twenty-nine years old, six years younger than Chris's real father would have been and two years younger than Chris's mother, seemed far and away the youngest of all the fathers there. He sat in the front passenger seat and was silent. It was a deliberate silence, within the tangible sphere of which he was wondering why exactly he had come. They were not far from their destination now. It seemed as though, around this bend, they might enter into a bigger light, a void into which they could disappear, where things would have trouble following them. He turned to his stepson.

"See any cars, Chris?"

Chris turned around in his seat to check the road in back of them again.

"No," he said.

The other boys in the back seat looked at Chris answering his father.

Mr. Gough snorted and roared: "Goddamn Wing drives like a goddamn ladybug! Goddamn Bray couldn't find this place even if he was already standing up to his knees in it!"

Chris studied Ian's face, but all expression was locked away from it; he was looking at his fellow passengers as though at a program on television. Whatever he saw did not satisfy him, apparently, and he looked out the window. In a few minutes, they seemed to have come to the horizon, the end of the world. The road swung abruptly to the right and on their left was the park entrance—a big, wide, dusty dirt road which led out onto the low hook of land.

It was a little after ten o'clock in the morning.

They drove between low dense trees, and so could not get a glimpse of the open water at either side.

Ian Davies had first lived in the vicinity of Waynesboro four years earlier, while on a nine-month assignment with the electronics corporation for which he still worked. The assignment was mostly an exercise in public relations, an effect of the joy it brought someone in an administrative department somewhere to play with names of people he'd never met and arrange them in a game of international musical chairs. Although Ian couldn't see what gain it brought the company to move him three thousand miles across the ocean and then back again, to carry on a bit of research in a windowless room that could as easily have been on one side of the Atlantic as the other, he succumbed quite happily to the experience. The pay was good (there was an increase of salary to induce employees to accept these assignments) and he had free lodging at a hotel until he could find a place to live. On top of that, there was an allowance for rent once a place was found, which puzzled Ian somewhat, but which he certainly didn't turn down.

As it turned out he hadn't had to do any househunting himself. His secretary, Mrs. Miro, a woman of about fifty, with arms that increased exponentially in circumference as they approached her shoulders and with hair that was dyed a reddish-orangeish ember color, did all that for him. His only role in the matter was to check out a place after she had found it. Several times she had taken him to see one, saying, "I wanted you to see it for yourself, I wouldn't take it if I were you, something better's bound to come up—" and so he would just look around and let Mrs. Miro smile and explain that "no, this isn't quite what we're looking for," leaving an intrigued landlord or landlady to try to puzzle out the relationship between the two of them.

Other times Mrs. Miro would come into his office and, shaking her arms, would cry, "Oh . . . you're going to love this!" (the way she talked, every syllable was pronounced and twisted in an accent that sounded to Ian Davies's ear meticulous yet foreign, but when he'd asked her where she came from, she had seemed to evade his question, answering, "Oh, from Elizabeth, Mr. Davies, right here in New Jersey, only now we're living in Stirling."), and then she'd take him to a brand-new development of apartments with built-in dishwashers, central air-conditioning, a swimming pool, tennis courts, and enormous amounts of space set aside for parking. He would smile vaguely all the way through the tour (there was an indoor gymnasium with a volleyball court too), convincing both Mrs. Miro and the superintendent that he was going to step into the real-estate office and sign a lease on the spot, until, on the way back to the car (Mrs. Miro drove him everywhere), he would either say, "I think I'd rather have something a little more homey, Mrs. Miro . . . " ("easy access" to a superhighway two hundred yards away hadn't appealed to him either) or "It's just a little bit too far from the office for me." He couldn't see himself traveling so far to work, some thirty or forty miles, as some of the executives in the London office did each day of the week, coming in from the Home Counties.

There appeared to be no hurry in finding a place to live. The hotel in Summit, where he was staying, was only four or five blocks from the train station, the train service was good, even on weekends, although the traincars were a far cry from British rail and not at all what he'd expected from America—they were ancient, with wicker seats and with rotary fans instead of the usual ubiquitous air-conditioning, and they ran along one of the roughest railbeds he'd ever experienced in his life. For a month or two he had a grand old time going into New York every Saturday or Sunday, seeing films and weekend matinees (everyone warned him against staying in New York after dark), going to museums, or just walking, looking at the neighborhoods. He even considered living in Manhattan and commuting. The company had its own bus taking employees from the city each day to the suburbs, where most of its offices had been relocated just a few years earlier. He started to sound out one of the younger men about it, a Mr. Byrne who he knew lived in the Village, but after one visit where he stayed overnight and Mr. Byrne revealed his true colors by trying to seduce Ian (no harm done) and another projected visit which had to be canceled because Mr. Byrne had just been mugged, Ian gave the idea up. He was happy as he was. He got invited to dinner at the house of one of the men at the office at least once or twice a week, and he became a weekly regular at a restaurant across the street from the train station in Summit. The hotel meals were fine for the rest of the week. He'd never lived so well before and he'd felt he'd be happy to stay at the hotel the whole nine months he'd be here, if no other suitable arrangement were to come to hand. The hotel suited the unreality of everything that was happening to him.

The thing that was odd about his enjoying it all so immensely was that for the first time in his life he was in a situation where there was absolutely no one he could relax with enough to say what he meant—confide, give observations. Things were so different here, taken much more seriously it seemed. Mr. Byrne, who had seemed an exception, always very forthcoming and friendly, eager to show Ian around the city, had, the week after the attempted seduction, been very standoffish and nervous whenever they met and Ian tried to say hello. Then, at the end of the week, he'd come up to Ian, obviously making a great effort, and said he was surprised but very grateful that Ian had taken the whole thing in his stride, which he, Mr. Byrne, certainly hadn't. It hadn't been at all like that with other members of the company whom he'd tried and sometimes even managed to seduce. Managing it, and seeing his victim the next day, was sometimes even worse than trying and failing— he spent whole afternoons, he said, being "paranoid" and taking long circuitous routes around the building just to avoid certain offices. He and Ian had arranged to get together for some jazz the next weekend, only that turned out to be the weekend poor Mr. Byrne got mugged, which left him so nervous that, as he explained to Ian on the phone, he didn't even want to answer his own doorbell.

Ian couldn't help wondering about Mr. Byrne; in England, at least in the crowd he'd run with in school and kept up with since then, any overture from a friend (Ian couldn't remember a time *he*'d ever really made an overture), whether male or female, had been met either with a "Thanks but no thanks" or a "Well . . . why not?" and it had been no big thing, until people started thinking they were in love, whereupon it became an unholy mess.

But things here didn't seem quite that simple. The lack of simplicity was somehow reflected in how all the couples whose houses he visited and who fed him meals seemed alike. Even the younger couples who would nonchalantly offer him marijuana instead of a drink (he couldn't help showing surprise the first time this happened) seemed to him very much out of the same mold as everyone else he met through the company. What was even stranger was that all their children, whether they were exquisitely or appallingly behaved, seemed to him to be alike — controlled by something bigger than themselves and about to go to pieces under the pressure of that control. He couldn't take any of the people he met as seriously as they took themselves, at least not on their own terms, and he felt this was not because he was callous or a cynic but because they were always play-acting, in simple predesignated terms, a happiness or a problem that remained entirely unconvincing. Really Mrs. Miro was the only one he began to feel at all close to, because unlike the others who, uninvited, told him everything randomly all the time about their personal lives without ever quite putting the information in focus (they talked like people who'd gone without any human contact for years and years), Mrs. Miro had to be asked about her life, and when she answered him she told it like a story and that gave it some weight. In general, he found himself attracted more to an older generation, their warmth seeming to him more natural, being drawn out of an initial reserve.

After close to three months in the hotel, Mrs. Miro found him a place to live, not through the real-estate office but through a private connection, so that there wouldn't be a fee or a lease, and six months would be a perfectly acceptable length of time to stay there. Her friend, Mrs. Castle, was a widow who lived in an old house in Waynesboro which was divided into three apartments, each with a separate entrance. She had a daughter-in-law and a grandson living in one apartment (the wife and son of Mrs. Castle's oldest boy, who had been killed "in the war"—Mrs. Miro didn't say which war) and, until recently, had had her youngest boy living in the third. He had just gotten married and moved out, however, leaving the apartment free, and both Mrs. Castle and the daughter-in-law thought it would be a good idea to have a man in the house. The rent would be reasonable, Waynesboro wasn't far from the office, and, upon meeting Mrs. Castle and seeing the house, Ian felt it would suit him exactly. He lost no time and moved in the following weekend.

Mrs. Castle was close to sixty years old. She had been born in Waynesboro and raised there. Her husband had too; they'd known each other all their lives, and had married once they'd graduated from high school. Then he'd gone to work in the post office. They'd had two boys. The oldest boy, Chrissie, had been a volunteer in the Marines. Chrissie had married, had a son, and then been killed the same week that his father died of a heart attack while on duty at the post office. What had made this double bereavement harder for Mrs. Castle to bear, oddly, was that there was a good possibility that neither of them ever knew of the other's death. Of course one of them, the one who died first, *had* not to know, and that was her son, not her husband. But in Mrs. Castle's mind the deaths became almost simultaneous because she'd kept Chrissie's death a secret for two days from her husband, and after two days the secret hadn't mattered anymore. It wasn't so much the actual pain of the deaths that lingered on and was unbearable (Mrs. Castle had always been a very practical woman, instinctively capable of handling the very worst, and not given to prolonged mourning—the shock was there and its reverberations lasted for years, but overt grief was short and sharp and not to be diminished by exaggeration). It was more a curiosity about her own behavior that began to haunt her, after the grief. Why had she kept a secret from her husband? It wasn't to protect him—or, if it was, it wasn't from any obvious need to do so. He hadn't been ill or depressed during the last two days he was alive. There'd been no warning whatsoever of any illness that would kill him. In his eyes, she must have behaved very unreasonably over those last two days, holding in a hostility and aggression that were aimed directly at him, as though he ought to have instinctively guessed her secret and was a fool for not being able to do so. Had he known? She had taken the phone call and teletyped message from the officials and then the phone call from Laura which had followed within an hour, all while her husband was at work. She couldn't think of any other source that he might have had the news from, but there was always the chance that a letter had been sent too and he'd intercepted it the way he sometimes did at the post office. That might even have been what had killed him. No letter was ever found on him, though, and no letter ever came. If he'd still been alive, even if unconscious with his eyes open, in the emergency room, she would have leaned down and told him:

"Chrissie's dead."

But he hadn't been. He had died in the ambulance on the way to the hospital. At the hospital, they performed an autopsy to see exactly what the problem had been. And it was simple—it had been his heart.

There was a double funeral, which Laura and little Chris came up for. Men in uniform were there along with an orator who said again and again that both men had died for their country. It was the first time that phrase had ever sounded absurd to her. It made her think a thought that she could never express to anyone, not even Laura. It seemed to her that, weighing it up, it wasn't her son (although, obviously, if it hadn't been for her son there would have been none of this military nonsense) but her husband who'd made the greater patriotic sacrifice: standing on his feet for thirty years, selling stamps and taking the abuse which the public loves to give post office workers.

Donald, her younger and now her only boy, went a little berserk in the middle of the eulogy and ran up and started beating on a soldier twice his size, until he was pulled away. She found herself thinking that if it weren't so sad, it might almost be funny: these men in uniform taking so seriously something they knew nothing about. Most of them were boys in basic training, probably. In the letters he'd sent, hadn't Chrissie's first newsworthy item, apart from the bad food and field exercises, been a military funeral? She couldn't even understand how this whole thing had been arranged. Somewhere along the line she must have said yes to someone she'd just wanted to get rid of. She'd always had the impression that military funerals were harder to come by.

Several weeks after the ceremony, Laura and Chris moved to Waynesboro from the Marine base where they'd been living. Laura's mother was alive and living in a small house in a rural town in Maryland, on the Delmarva Peninsula, but there was no easy possibility of doing there what Laura had to do now—acquire a skill of some sort and get a job. Waynesboro was a better place for that. She got a Marine pension for a while, as well as free room and board and free babysitting from Mrs. Castle, and so was able to take an intensive training course at a local business college for a year and then get a secretarial position at a real-estate office in Waynesboro at just the time when real estate was beginning to pick up there. Donald graduated from high school and went to work as a garage mechanic, cars being something he had always been good at. They all stayed on at the house, and during the summer when Chris turned three and Donald and Laura started working and money got a little less tight, the three of them (with the help of a local carpenter, Mr. Berringer) worked on converting the house into three apartments, while Chris sat on the lawn and followed their activity, occasionally pointing out where someone had left and forgotten a hammer or a box of nails. Whenever the level wasn't being used, Chris had it, holding it up in his hands and trying to balance it and keep the bubble in the green liquid steady.

It was six years after this that Ian moved in and, after a few weeks, found himself spending quite a bit of time with Laura—sometimes accompanied by Chris, sometimes without Chris. On weekends they drove to parks, to Hacklebarney or Jockey Hollow, for a walk and for Ian to see the place where George Washington had camped out. Once or twice they drove into New York. On week nights they'd occasionally go to a restaurant in Waynesboro which they both liked. Ian told her about England and offered to put her up if she were ever to go there.

Laura had never been outside the States, and even her travel within the States had been restricted to the limited view offered from various Marine bases, which all seemed alike. Over the six years since her husband had died, she'd gone out with very few men, mostly old friends of Chrissie's still living in Waynesboro who dropped by on occasion, although not so often as they had before Chrissie had joined the Marines. They all liked old Mrs. Castle and they all felt a little put on the spot when, in the middle of a conversation, Mrs. Castle would suddenly pick up a newspaper, find a movie that was just about to start, and rush whoever it was and Laura off to it, without going herself.

Laura found herself having so little in common with these old friends of Chrissie's that she began to wonder how much common ground she might have had with Chrissie himself. They'd both been very young when they'd run off and gotten married—she'd only just grad-uated from high school. And, after a brief honeymoon, she'd only seen him sporadically, during periods of leave. He'd been killed just after their third anniversary, which they'd had to spend apart. The memory of each of her encounters with him, isolated as they were by long periods of separation, left her wondering if he really had been what she had seen in him. Months of being alone in a compound for junior officers' wives, first pregnant, and then with a baby to take care of, had forced her in on herself and started her thinking. She'd worked her way systematically through the library of every base she stayed at, finding that when the baby was quiet she wanted to be quiet too, rather than listen to records or look at television the way she used to.

Every time Chrissie had come back, she had felt as though she were seeing a different thing, coming more and more into focus, and she wasn't at all sure that she liked what she saw, partly because it was tied up with a growing suspicion of her own folly in choosing to marry so young and partly just because of Chrissie himself. He left her wondering what perfect image she must be comparing him with. It was possible that that image was her father's, she supposed (pop psychology books were only too eager to point this out), although all she had of her father was a few memories and some of the family's stock anecdotes, which had been passed down in terms which were (she was realizing) a little too homey, a little too vivid, a little less creditable and a little less sufficient than she had previously been led to believe—like a word which she had used or abused for the better part of her life before beginning to wonder what it meant, being so integral a part of her vocabulary.

When the news came of Chrissie's death, it was a shock not so much because of her own personal loss (although that, in a dry-eyed kind of way, hit her harder than she'd ever expected) but because it was the closest Death had ever come to her (she had been too young and he had been too far away for her to have known it when her father had been killed) and also because whatever else he might have been, Chrissie had been alive, more alive than anyone else she could think of. There had been no containing him, and it seemed odd that that force could in any way have withdrawn from him, almost like a person with great poise and self-possession suddenly having a carpet pulled out from underneath him and taking an ungainly fall. What she found she wanted after his death was an escape which wasn't offered in Chrissie's Waynesboro friends, all of whom were several years older than she was. Because she was quiet, they tended to treat her as though she must be stupid, and they talked about Chrissie in a way that made her like him less with every detail.

Ian Davies was closer to her in age and she found herself talking with him under no pressure whatsoever about things that interested her and apparently interested him too. The only thing that puzzled her in her contact with him was why the question of sex never came up—it seemed part of a prohibition that he rather than she had imposed. Both her mother-in-law and Chris liked him and felt relaxed with him too, and by the end of six months the four of them had grown very close, almost like a family—a family without its dark side yet. He had meals with them, bought presents for Chris, took Mrs. Castle out to dinner and a show at the Papermill Playhouse when it was her birthday and, in short, was the gentleman—attentive, pleasant to look at, pleasant to be with. On his part, Ian enjoyed this time spent at the house in Waynesboro better than he'd enjoyed anything since university. Memories from university had soured a little or grown thin. Many of his friends had married, and although he still visited them occasionally, most of the meetings seemed awkward juggling acts—trying to strike a balance between getting back to an old intimacy with an old friend (largely through an insistent reminiscence which made it seem as though all his life was going to be meaningful only in retrospect), while taking desperate care not to exclude a spouse who, no matter how he fought it, always seemed to him very much like an inexplicably jealous stranger suddenly appeared on the scene.

What he liked about the Castles was that they all appeared to be living in the present, which, even if it wasn't very interesting, was pleasant enough. Perhaps the reason that they didn't reminisce, although Ian had the outline of the family story from both Laura and Mrs. Castle within a few weeks of meeting them, was that the presence of a tragedy rather than a mere series of adventures could leave no doubt as to the past's irreclaimability. It also appealed to him that no one of them seemed to dominate the others and none of them put an exclusive claim on his, Ian's, interest. If they were all four in a room together, he could talk and spend time with any one of them, Laura, Chris, or Mrs. Castle, without feeling he was leaving anyone out. It was odd, but in a very short time the four of them worked better as a unit than anything Ian had ever known. Perhaps because he had been an only child, he had always found his own family a little claustrophobic—so much attention was focused on him, for lack of any other focus.

When it was time for him to leave Waynesboro, he was very sorry to go. In his bachelor digs in Basingstoke he felt much more isolated than he'd thought of himself as being before he'd left for the States. Friends he saw joked that he'd picked up a Yankee accent and then remarked between themselves afterward, with some surprise, that he seemed even quieter than before— they'd thought the States might open him up some.

Two months went by and the Castles had no word from Ian. Laura continued at her job, Chris was in school, and Mrs. Castle stayed at home tending house, tidying what didn't need to be tidied. They all felt a gap, although they couldn't describe it. It was as though Ian, by not being there, had left them with nothing to say to each other. The mailbox at the end of the driveway was checked each day for a brief but tactful letter that would address each one of them individually, without necessarily calling them by name (there would be an evenly delegated quantity of details designed to strike a peculiar recognition in the mind of each of the recipients in turn), and give its news, asking for a reply in return.

But no letter came and, while the idea of Ian came a little clearer as the weeks passed and he began to form into an image which they could fondly refer to and tell anecdotes about, a doubt also began to rise as to whether they'd gotten the idea right at all. If they'd been asked at the moment of his leaving what they'd expected to happen as far as keeping up the tie, they would have said, knowing what they did of Ian, that a regular, informative correspondence gradually tailing off into annual Christmas cards would be the most likely possibility. They thought of Ian as doing things regularly, rather than in bursts. But the arising doubt that they had wasn't so much whether they had got Ian "right" as to how good a correspondent he might be, but whether Ian had really cared for them the way they'd felt he had. And the ensuing silence after departure left just enough room for that doubt to grow.

Then on a Friday night, more than two months after he had left, they heard from him: he made a transatlantic phone call. He talked to Laura for a while and then to Mrs. Castle for almost twenty minutes. When she pointed out the cost to him, he answered that he had nothing else to do with his money, did he? and he asked for Chris. Then he asked Chris for Laura again and, after talking for a long time aimlessly about nothing in particular, he asked Laura point-blank without leading up to it at all if she would like to marry him. Chris and Mrs. Castle overheard and understood from Laura's response what was suddenly going on, and the thing that added to the surprise of it, apart from the odd timing involved, was the fact that the proposal was coming over the telephone. During his months with them in Waynesboro, Ian had never once made a phone call (he hadn't had a phone installed), and whenever he did, on rare occasions, get a business call at Laura's or Mrs. Castle's (Mrs. Miro appeared to have had no qualms about giving the two numbers out), he'd never let the conversation last beyond three minutes. It added to the confusion to have such a momentous turn of events come via an instrument that, really, it was hard to connect with Ian at all.

Laura asked him to let her have the weekend to think it over and it was arranged that Ian would call again the following Monday. The main reason he wanted to marry her, apart from his liking her and enjoying her company, seemed to be that he felt so comfortable with her mother-in-law and Chris, and she wanted time to think over whether this struck her as a legitimate reason. When she mentioned her surprise that he'd used the phone rather than written her a letter, he said that it was just another sign of his being "Americanized," and the joke rang oddly false. It had been a good joke when they'd all four gone out to a Dairy Queen or all the way to Route 22 for a drive-in movie because that was the nearest one and Ian wanted to see one before he left the States. It had been the first time any of them had seen one but it had been Ian, as they'd all said, who by seeing it was getting "Americanized."

If the joke sounded false now, then it was partly because he was nervous, but it seemed to her partly for some other reason too. She wondered if he had been thinking about marriage while he'd still been in the States. She didn't have the nerve to ask him about it, but she wanted time to think about that possibility and the implication of his not having brought up the question *then*. The other thing to take into consideration was that if they wanted to marry right away, which seemed to be what they were talking about, it would involve Laura and Chris's moving to England, since Ian appeared to have no immediate prospect of returning to the States on assignment. Moving to England would mean taking Chris out of school and Laura giving up her job. It would also mean leaving Mrs. Castle in the house in Waynesboro on her own, and that was a worry to Laura, even if Mrs. Castle gave the impression to everybody else that she could take care of herself. Mrs. Castle had given Laura shelter and company when she had needed it, and Laura felt she owed Mrs. Castle some company if nothing else.

She went over most of these points with her mother-in-law, who perhaps gave her more assurance than she really wanted as to Ian's being steady and "safe," and then she asked Chris if he would like to move to England and if he would mind interrupting his school year and starting in another school, maybe an English school, saying that they could certainly wait if he wanted to. But Chris appeared not to mind anything, and when Ian called back on the Monday night, she said yes she would marry him and come to England, and they immediately began to make arrangements for her and Chris to move there. They also booked a round-trip flight for Mrs. Castle, who was coming along for the wedding and for a vacation.

The actual trip there was the thing that stuck most in Chris's mind whenever he thought of the circumstances that had put him in this new relation to Ian. The thing he'd liked best, looking down from the plane as it flew over the southern tip of Greenland, had been the ice floes. He'd been able to see an eggshell surface of ice cracking apart and, in the way it broke, the pattern of the currents which forced it to break. Landing had been strange, too, seeing for the first time a place which had fields but hardly any woods—a whole country which looked like a wrinkled patchwork quilt done in greens which glowed brighter and were more pervasive than any greens in Waynesboro.

Ian met them at Heathrow and then took them down by car to his parents' house in Brockenhurst, in the New Forest, where there was room to put them up. After introductions and a day or two's rest, there really wasn't much vacation for anyone involved. First there was the wedding, which was held in a registrar's office, with Mrs. Castle and the Davieses and one of Ian's old university friends for witnesses. This was followed immediately by some rather frenzied househunting. Mrs. Davies, Laura, Mrs. Castle, and Chris constituted the hunting party (Ian and his father both had to work—old Mr. Davies taught botany and zoology at a "tech" in Southampton), and in the late afternoon, after each day's search and visiting of real-estate offices, they would call it a day and Mrs. Davies would lead them to an obscure teashop which she always seemed to know of (Laura began to build up an image of Mrs. Davies's life as an endless wandering from town to town, across the south of England, in search of a good cup of tea) where Chris could eat lots of crumpets and scones and wash them down with orange squash. He seemed to have fallen in perfectly happily with the move (his main comment being "Look how small," pointing to row houses or cottages or gardens or streets that were tucked into some corner of the landscape in great contrast to the general sprawl in the layout of suburban Waynesboro), and the Davieses seemed genuinely to like both Chris and Laura.

There had naturally been apprehension on both sides at first, the Davieses' apprehension being that an American woman and a nine-year-old American boy would possibly be an embarrassment both in public and with certain old friends of theirs. Laura's apprehension had been simply a worry that she and Chris wouldn't be accepted, either because of their being American or because of her previously having been not just married but married to an American Marine with a nine-year-old boy which put her obviously older than Ian. Anti-Vietnam feeling was still running high at that time, and any understanding of the plight of the ordinary American in that situation was not often forthcoming. Any American tended, instead, to be a scapegoat.

She sensed, too, that the Davieses were perhaps a little more proper than they considered it possible that she or Chris or Mrs. Castle could be. But the anticipated social embarrassment came, unexpectedly, on Mrs. Davies's side in an odd exchange that was prompted by a conversation between Mrs. Castle and Mrs. Davies, the week before Mrs. Castle went back to the States, while they were in Southampton.

All of the High Street in Southampton was new, made of concrete and glass ("like our malls," Mrs. Castle had said), except for the Bargate, which stood on its own more like a rock, a volcanic outcrop, than something man had made, it was so much in contrast to what men made now. This had led to Mrs. Castle's asking what Southampton had been like before the war and where Mrs. Davies had been at the time, which led to Mrs. Davies's talking about being a hospital volunteer in the early days of the war, at the hospital where she'd met her husband.

They had all listened, the story had held everyone's interest, until she'd started to end it in an odd way, suddenly addressing Laura more than Mrs. Castle and saying, " . . . which is why I feel sorry for you, your generation, having nothing to hold you together." But which generation did she mean? Laura, if anything, felt very much between generations or, if not between, then outside of her own, a generation which could not tolerate the least aberration, whether fated or willed, from its streamlined pattern. Mrs. Davies had gone on, "It's an awful thing to say, but we had the war. Nothing's felt quite so right as how we all acted together then, nothing since then has been quite so easy to understand . . . as the war was. . . . "

She had paused and looked at Laura as though the meaning and lesson of this statement ought to be clear for Laura to see and act upon, but Laura had had only to look back at her, without saying a word and with Chris sitting next to her much quieter (it suddenly struck Mrs. Davies) than a boy his age ought to be, to make it perfectly clear that nothing could have been much more in contrast than the two women's (three, really, including Mrs. Castle) respective wars, as far as pulling together or an easy understanding was concerned. A tension between Mrs. Davies and Laura lasted through the rest of that afternoon and evening, and it wasn't until late that night, while Ian was talking with his father and Chris was in bed, that Mrs. Davies, on a prompting from Mrs. Castle, was able to find Laura alone and make both an apology and a foray of sorts into Laura's reason for marrying her son.

This little exchange put the women on a more equal footing, as though their two mistakes had led to their recognition of the same thing: each other's basic worth. Mrs. Davies's mistake had been an obvious one of tact. But Laura's was less obvious, having more to do with an error in judgment as to the kind of escape that she had perhaps thought she could achieve in marrying Ian and even in moving to England. If she'd thought she could escape her country and the messages it sent out, or the real sacrifices it demanded in the name of imagined or exaggerated differences or points of honor, she had been wrong. Every meeting with the idea of England in the abstract (which she'd come across in Ian several times but overlooked and which was what her exchange with Ian's mother had been all about) only put into sharper definition her relation to her own country and what its demands on her had so far been. Mrs. Davies inadvertently had led to this recognition in the least painful way possible and with a frankness which Laura doubted it would have occurred to an American of the same generation to use without using it to say something else more personal and irrelevant and unpleasant. An American would have suggested blame, as though the war and being a single mother and anti-patriotic feeling could all be piled up on her head as the consequence of her generation's character. That had been her experience, at any rate, and she was grateful to Mrs. Davies for immediately seeing through the absurdity of blame after her first blunder.

Ian's father remained somewhat of a mystery to Laura—occasionally, through startling resemblances to his son, alerting her to how much of a mystery Ian was to her too. Chris liked old Mr. Davies, however, who was always showing him things—mostly plants and insects —and explaining them to him, taking an interest in Chris which no man Mr. Davies's age had taken before. Chris hadn't had a grandfather.

The house which Ian and Laura eventually took was in Winchester, where they lived for the next three years. They were near the station so Ian could take a train to work, and they weren't far from Southampton and Ian's parents. Chris went to an English school. In winter, when there weren't so many tourists, Winchester reminded Laura of the small town on the Delmarva peninsula where she'd grown up and where her mother lived still, and also of Mrs. Castle's descriptions of Waynesboro before the suburbs had encroached upon it.

They had three holidays while they lived in England. The first was one up to Scotland. The second was a bicycling holiday in Holland. At the end of three years they found out Ian was going to be transferred back to the States again, so they made plans for a holiday in France which they'd been thinking about for a long time—a trip to Brittany and to Normandy, to the war beaches where Laura's father was supposed to be buried. The first few days of the holiday, however, were spent with Ian's parents in Brockenhurst, after which they planned to get the boat from Southampton.

The afternoon before they left was cool and dry and clear, and Ian's father drove them over to the Beaulieu aerodrome, where they walked around. They were on a flat heath which, although it wasn't more than two hundred feet above sea level, gave the impression of being the high flat top of the world. To the south, across the Solent, they could see the fields of the Isle of Wight rise up into the air. The day was so clear that they could see a sharp searing point of light when the sun was caught and reflected for a moment on a car's fender, although they couldn't see the car itself as it traveled along one of the roads on the island.

All around them, on this heath, abandoned runways followed a geometric pattern and were overgrown and cracked apart by heather and gorse, which were taking over everything. Grass came up, too, through the cracks in the concrete. There was a hill (made of leftover sand

and gravel for concrete, dumped here thirty years ago) which you could climb up to see the pattern of the runways better. That pattern looked as forlorn and once-meaningful as the excavated foundations of Roman villas where you can just barely see the outline of how Romans would have walked from one room to another. Chris liked it up there and turned around and around. He stood next to old Mr. Davies. His mother and Ian were up there too and walked a little way away, but Chris could still hear what they were saying:

"Maybe this is it. . . . " His mother's voice was vague. "It sounds just like the one in the letter."

"Might have been anywhere, actually—they've got them like this all along the coast down to Dover," his stepfather answered.

Then they all climbed back down and walked across the heath to where a ring of birch trees surrounded a perfectly round pond six or seven feet in diameter and absolutely still. There wasn't any mud, but only gravel at its bottom and thrown up in a ring around it too, like a protective barrier. The wind made a sound in the birch trees like the whistle of a harp. You didn't even know there was a pond there until you climbed the ring and were on top of it. Ian's father, once they all had their attention focused on it and had fallen into silence, pointed directly at it, laughed as though it were the private source of all his amusement, and said, "Bombhole"— where a bomb had landed thirty years before, blown a pockmark in the sandy soil, filled with water . . . and filled with water, still, whenever it rained for more than a day or two.

Then he led them off again and Laura felt as though she were about to have a confrontation with him the way she'd had one with his wife several years earlier.

She could tell when a poke of some sort at the difference
between them, at her being American, was being led up
to, and it felt like he was leading up to a poke now. For
the first time she felt like having a poke back at him, she
felt in the right shape for it, about to go back home. Ian
smiled at her because he knew what was coming next
and he thought Chris would like it, which might mean
that Laura and his father would close a little more of the
gap between them—at least, Ian thought of it as a gap.
His father and Laura had still never gotten into a serious
conversation, for which his father was largely responsible
because right from the start old Mr. Davies had believed
Laura incapable of it, and Laura, sensing this and feeling
that it badly underestimated her, had refused to put
herself out and make any unusual effort to prove him
wrong, for which Ian couldn't blame her. Trying to
argue a case that shouldn't need arguing would only
seem to make the case weaker. He found it harder to
understand why Laura resented the fact that everything
—Irish murders, coal strikes, Mid-East crises—had the
air of keeping his father endlessly amused. He chuckled
over them while he mounted his specimens. That was
almost a source of secret relief for Ian and, contrary to
what Laura thought—that the laughter was strange
and cold—it seemed to Ian that the laughter was the
only thing that gave the atrocity life, gave it its due. If
there was one thing he felt he had learned from his
father, if only because of the double edge and the inner
tension it involved, it was that no murder was complete
without laughter. He reckoned nothing would haunt a
murderer so and nothing would make clearer what the
murder might mean than your laughing in his face.

Old Mr. Davies was leading them along a winding taxi
strip where the gorse grew high on either side, making it

like a maze. He had a hand on Chris's shoulder, guiding him, as it were, although it was perfectly obvious where to go—there was no choice. They came around one bend, and then another, working toward a point where the heath changed abruptly into farmers' fields with thick hedgerows demarking them, and then they stopped.

Ian's father directed Chris's attention with a nod.

"Look—"

Chris looked, and just as he had thought it might, Ian saw the same kind of smile break over his father's and Chris's face. Laura stood behind them.

They had come to a spot where the taxi strip just disappeared with a surreal effect into the hedgerow, obviously continuing but no longer followable—like a road Ian and Chris had seen on one of their first excursions together in New Jersey, to a reservoir; a road which went underwater where it used to be dry, the yellow stripe down the middle fading into algae-green and, farther off, the shine of reflected blue.

Ian's father continued to look at the hedgerow and then looked at Laura. His eyes met her eyes and he could see that this was neither what she had expected nor what she hadn't expected, it was neither of the things she was braced for, but something off to the side which failed to click at all. He failed to see what Ian saw in her and, once again, a doubt he had about Ian was a little more enforced, and it occurred to him to wonder how happy Chris could really be. He looked at the boy and realized from the abstracted gaze on his face that Chris could be thinking of nothing or anything. Disappointed, then, he leaned away from the three of them, as though to examine more closely a flower or a vine tangled in the gorse where none was to be seen and, speaking aloud to no one in particular, finished what he'd started saying. "—a road that goes nowhere."

"Hangman's noose," Mr. Berringer announced again.

And then he put it away. He looked around and grinned at the three boys in the back seat, especially at Anthony Wing; he looked inquisitively at Anthony as a bird does at the dirt while it remembers what a worm is or, if it's a hawk (which was closer to what Mr. Berringer might be), what shape a rabbit makes when it bounds in terror, pursued by a shadow, across a field. Mr. Berringer's look addressed all concerned, even Mr. Bray, and it asked: Did they remember the knot? Had the knot left a shape in their minds? What did they think of it? Or were they thinking, already, of something else?

Mr. Bray had carried on only one exit beyond the one which would have taken them to Sandy Hook before he realized his mistake, but it had taken a while to find a place where they could pull off the highway, get over to the other side, and reverse their direction. There were myriad signs—billboards, road signs, in every color, size, and lettering, some of them neon and flashing, announcing prices, various kinds of entertainment, directions—and they all combined to make Mr. Bray feel very nervous, as if he were driving through a whirling, shifting kaleidoscope or were at home stranded in the midst of his family's constant inspired grievance and confusion. Just as with his family, where he could not tell genuine grievances from gratuitous disruptions, so on this highway he could not tell helpful directions— *Exit 18 . . . 1/2 mile . . . Keep in right hand lane*—from gratuitous exploitative directions—*Buy two . . . get one free . . . Exit 200 yards*—and this put him in a panic.

The sun was bright, the sky was blue, but these were things that did not help him out of his confusion; they were almost mirrors.

After he had made a U-turn and pointed the car back north toward the Sandy Hook exit, he pulled into the parking lot of a diner, parked the car, turned the engine off, and then sat with his arms folded over the steering wheel and his eyes staring forlornly at the view of fast and slow lanes in front of him. For a few moments no one said anything. Billy Bray said nothing because he knew this parking and silence to be an integral part of his father's ritual of being lost or temporarily astray from the direct route, and however much he might ridicule other aspects of his father's character and behavior, whether openly or behind his back, both he and his twin brother still had a profound respect for this "being-lost" routine.

And, because Billy Bray seemed to find the situation and silence perfectly acceptable, Anthony Wing and Chuckie Massie did too; Anthony didn't even say that he had to go to the bathroom, but instead sat quieter than any of them. To all three boys it seemed that they couldn't really call the place where they were right now "lost" (unless being "lost" was just another name for a privilege) because after all here they were seeing things which boys in the other cars wouldn't have seen and which could be told about when the separated parties were reunited: "There's a Howard Johnson's and there's not so many trees, *that* way," giving out a direction toward which they could point with confidence.

Mr. Berringer, however, wasn't fully clued in on this way of seeing Mr. Bray's driving and navigational efforts. These seemed like blank and wasted moments to him; so he pulled out his bit of cord again and began working on another knot with which to test the boys. Mr. Bray sighed. An interesting bird fluttered down onto the hood of the car and then fluttered off again, off to the side, toward a high pile of used tires behind a service station next to the diner. Mr. Bray leaned over, opened his glove compartment, and extracted from it a map, which he opened up and then refolded so that he had the lower half of Staten Island and the upper corner of the Jersey shore, with the Raritan Bay and River in between, in view. Roads were black or red or gray, thick and thin, depending on what kind of road it was; a variety of logos announced the locations of various service stations, Holiday Inns, and local airports. The sea was a baby-blue on the map, and it was close by, it was all around — it appeared to prevent the roads from going any farther. That did not so much make Mr. Bray nervous as it made him feel depressed and wonder if he was going to die soon. He folded up the map. He put it back in the glove compartment. Then he looked out the front windshield again and the side windows of the car, as though tallying what he had seen on the map with what he could see all around him.

Discarded railway ties had been used to separate this parking lot from the highway. A fringe of weeds grew out from under the ties. The sun was bright and the sky was too, like a longing for sleep.

Mr. Bray was blank ("At least the boys are behaving well," he thought in some far-off corner of his mind, not taking into account how surprising it would have been if this particular combination of boys in the back seat were to choose to misbehave, since none of them was likely to find the other two an inspiration for mischief) and Mr. Berringer was busy, absorbed — with ropes and fingers, ropes and fingers. He looked up in surprise when Mr. Bray turned on the ignition; he sat up in his seat in further surprise when, with some force and determination, Mr. Bray pulled out of the sorry half-gravel, half-asphalt paving of the parking lot onto the smoother surface of the parkway and picked up speed.

But then he went back to his knot and it was as though there were no connection between him and the world. He could talk directly to boys, to children. He could frighten them, arouse their curiosity, and send messages with enormous gaps in them which they could only try to fill in with reverence or contempt. After all, he was almost an old man. To a much greater extent than any of the other men on this camping trip, he had done what he had meant to do. Retrospect was beginning to have almost all the weight with him. Surprise was a thing he mimed with perfection. As if he had once again managed to astonish himself, he held the new knot up for them all to see, announced its name—"Turk's head"—and then grinned. Billy Bray looked openly bored with it, while Anthony Wing looked terrified, and Chuckie Massie (who was feeling just a little bit carsick) stared at the knot in a blank idiot stupor. This made Mr. Berringer abruptly shut his mouth into a flat straight line. His other look, of melancholy, fell over his face and made him look like a monkey or a cat who doesn't understand.

In similar circumstances, his own boys' reactions could not have been much more different from the reactions of these three. His own boys, the Berringer boys, could never in their lives have looked bored or in a stupor, and though they could look shy, deferential, they could never in their lives have given themselves over to abject terror the way any of the Wings could. His own boys, whenever they wandered into his workshop to tell him something or to ask him something, would at least, when he finally

looked up from what he was doing and noticed them
and grinned, accept the grin. His own boys knew how to
accept what was offered. There was never any outward
expression or dramatization of acceptance, their faces
were almost wooden, but you could tell that now, from
this particular moment, the grin and whatever else went
with it would be inside them, there to draw on, tying in
with part of a bigger thing. It would be used, shyly at
first, with friends; and then in a year or two (first by
Blue the older, then by Clay two years younger) on
women; but the grin's real moment would come in twenty,
in thirty years' time when they would use it on *their*
sons and have it catch, see its meaning catch. The
Berringer boys, when you thought of them, made you
think of wood, but of fabulous wood, hardwood, wood
invested with a fragrance, small sturdy oaks which with
age would turn to wiry oaks, tangled, contorted, perverse,
but always strong, with each secret shape they made, in
their trunk, in the grain inside them, like the shape of
the grin, hidden or manifest, whichever it was.

The Berringer boys were like Mr. Berringer's ultimate
trick on the world, fathered when he was in his late
forties and now silently going about their business,
when he was past sixty. You could look at them and
then at their progenitor and think they were a thing the
old man had invented right on the spot. Or that they
were a trick played, not on the world, but on Mrs.
Berringer, who after fifteen years of married life hadn't
expected children, had been slim like a rod fitting perfectly
into changelessness, into sameness, when along came
her boys and now, fifteen years later, here *she* was—
huge, vast, but still gentle, with the movements of a
woman who has the mind of being slim. There were
occasions when she still couldn't quite credit her own or

her sons' appearance—her sons seemed unknown to
themselves, like beings snatched from another planet or
orbiting off into a dream. There was something about
them that seemed their father's specific intention, his
achievement, like a consummately built and mysteriously
captivating cabinet. Every time they noticed something,
they noticed it suddenly, as though neither they nor it
had been there all along. And really, no couple could
have asked for more in the way of children than what
the Berringers had gotten with their boys, who were
courteous, sensitive, practical, responsible, and, although
not handsome in the usual sense (they had crooked
noses, drawn-in chins and vague unfocused eyes), always
interesting to look at.

Mr. Bray thought of them with longing and despair,
for if Mr. Berringer appeared at this point to be going at
just a slightly higher and more mischievous speed than
that of his sons, whose speeds were still locked into
dreams (only two days ago Clay's teacher had sent a
note home, suggesting that father and son might want
to have a word with each other; for the past week,
during history period, Clay had been trying to inflate
his sweater by blowing into one sleeve while holding the
other sleeve closed, something she had never before
seen anyone attempt to do), then the Bray twins were
miles, were light-years beyond the poky irresolute pace
of their father. How had he ever produced them? How
had he ever mustered the speed to get them going?

Mr. Bray was thirty-seven; almost all the hair had
left his head and he was gaining weight. His frame was
elongated and slight and didn't carry his weight well, so
that he looked like a scarecrow covered in sandbags or
swamped in a lack of meaningful definition. The Bray
twins had just turned fourteen, were lithe and slender,

they had blond-white hair, gazelle faces, and eyes so blue and crystalline they almost hurt with energy — you could look at old photographs of Mr. Bray and see he had been just like them as far as looks went when he was a boy. But he might well have been, judging from his quiet stance in picture after picture (looking always as if he had accidentally appeared and, due to embarrassment, was longing to fade or retreat back into whatever scenery constituted the background), a more timid, less outgoing sort than either of his sons. He had been one of those boys who let another boy initiate him into everything. In Mr. Bray's case, this other boy had been Bill Jewitt, and the climax of these initiations had come in the summer between his senior year in high school and his first year in college, a summer filled with stupendous alcoholic adventures and a constant earnest distortion of women into bizarre and remote, temperamental, otherworldly creatures, whose desirability and formidability were both exaggerated in order to excuse the paralyzing shyness both boys, but especially Mr. Bray, came up against in approaching them. Like the alcohol, this invocation of "woman" was a ritual and it had its counterpart in the cheerleaders' dressing room or in preponderantly female households where the males of the high school were assessed and arranged in a hierarchy in which the ultimate praise was to be acknowledged as "cute" (boys had it made if it could also be added that they were "sweet"), while the ultimate damnation was to be deemed "gross" or "weird." The boys, of course, similarly categorized the girls, and for those at the top of both lists the system worked admirably well without its ever having to be thought about. Since Mr. Bray had been not only "cute" but "sweet," he had hardly had to lift a finger or direct a glance before he found himself over his head in situations which he couldn't even recognize enough specifically as "situations" to know if he wanted to escape them, let alone consider how he could honorably escape if escape was what he found he wanted. In that miracle of childhood training which goes into producing an American male, he had arrived at adolescence a perfect cipher, locked into an innocent acceptance of an ostensibly innocent world—an acceptance which, if one can maintain it throughout life, withstanding or avoiding and ignoring a variety of pressures and revelations from without and within, can lead to a continuum of experience so bland, so unvarying, so Christian (when viewed in the terms of a small country community, which Oldminster, the town where Mr. Bray had grown up, had been not so long ago) that it has no shape at all, as if two perfectly good eyes had opened, never looked to the right or to the left but only straight ahead, onto an empty sky with no birds, observed and tallied nothing for the requisite sixty-five or seventy-two years, without blinking, before they had their lids pressed shut—and were buried. Perhaps the deepest question (what are the colors of the flag? what are the names of the planets? what is the capital of Montana?) would be a multiple choice for which years of school training would have prepared one: *The color of the sky is: A—Red; B—Green; C—Yellow; D—Blue.* Of course the answer was *D—Blue.* It had been mentioned repeatedly in books: *D—Blue.* Mr. Bray would take a girl out in his father's car tonight, park in a dark place, lean over, and whisper, "The sky is *D—Blue.*" Mr. Bray was, in fact, the typical product of a people who had invested their faith not so much in the actual weave of a moral fabric as in the starch which kept that fabric stiff, unpliable, and, ultimately, unworkable, self-defeating—totally impractical.

Given this social context, Mr. Bray had the additional shortcomings of being uncertain of himself and of being by nature kind. He was kind to animals and, although he was totally unaware of it, he was more comfortable with animals than with human beings. If he was at a party and there was a choice between meeting an animal, a dog or cat for instance, or meeting a human being, he always chose the animal. These shortcomings of uncertainty and kindness made him perhaps the most attractive male in the whole high school, but they were the final straws in undermining his ability to cope realistically with any human situation at all. That he was uncertain of himself led him to want to control things, and that he was kind by nature led him to want things to be under his control by their own volition, the whole situation, ideally, imbued with a feeling of blithe, purposeful generosity—and it was in perfect innocence and hopeful-ness that he desired all this to be. It was with utter incomprehension that he watched things go along and fail to move toward this end. An additional burden was to be found in the fact that despite his having failed to master certain presumably masculine qualities of arro-gance, bravado, and self-interest, he was somehow unable to desire something other than the things with which those qualities are rewarded. His association with Bill Jewitt didn't help matters. It made him out to be, like Bill, a bit of a rogue; while confused encounters with various members of a clique of cheerleaders led the girls to label him "fickle"—a label which confused him because he didn't know how it was intended. His reputation was further enhanced by Bill's vivid descriptions of him drunk and vomiting out the door of a tent in the early hours of the morning in woods outside town, so that, helpless and shy as he was, the girls couldn't help being drawn to him. And the boys liked him too. They respected him because he was good-looking and managed hardly ever to say anything, while never giving the impression of creating distance or being stuck-up.

Had Mr. Bray ever been in love? Had he ever been happy?

He might have been happy that one summer, between high school and college. At eighteen, life can still have an effortless definitive hallucinatory quality which somehow comes across as the "main thing"; and, although there are no real words to describe or attach to the experience, one can see perfectly, in brief intense moments, physical things as they are with an almost excruciating precision which is both exhilarating and harrowing. Even vomiting is a desolate pleasure, if done with a friend and in an atmosphere of absolute freedom and abandon. To be dead drunk outdoors, in woods, in summer, looking up into the sky and smelling the earth, is incomparable. There were certain moments, simple views of stars seen through the foliage of trees and an alcoholic haze, that were destined to remain an epicenter of Mr. Bray's existence. It was perhaps in a kind of homage to these moments that Mr. Bray, tired as he was, had helped conduct scout camping trips for the past three years. So, yes, he had been happy.

Love was a different question. Certainly Mr. Bray thought he had been in love. At college he had studied business economics and, throughout his freshman year, had been terribly homesick and lonely. Then, during his sophomore year, he had met his future wife, a girl from Waynesboro, which was a small town not far from Oldminster, and he had concentrated on her, he had managed to fall in love with her. She, in turn, had concentrated on him, managed to respond to his love.

He proposed to her and she accepted him and so they were engaged. They told their parents and their parents protested. They threatened to go right on ahead and get married and their parents threatened to withhold funds. They got married anyway (it was the most exciting and daring thing either of them had ever done) and their parents went ahead and financed them through their junior and senior years.

During the winter term of their senior year, Mrs. Bray became pregnant. They both got their degrees in business, went for a brief honeymoon in Bermuda (again, their parents footed the bill), returned to Waynesboro, and moved into a garage apartment owned by Mr. Bray's father-in-law, for which they paid only a nominal rent. Mr. Bray got a job in the local bank. Mrs. Bray had the twins prematurely in the middle of August, and although circumstances were pinched at first, Mr. Bray did well in his job and within a few years was earning enough to keep his family comfortably.

In their timing of things, they were very lucky. When Mr. Bray had joined the bank, Waynesboro was still a small town with not more than five or six thousand inhabitants and with two or three villages of not more than two or three hundred residents each within a three-mile radius of it—this constituted the township. However, spreading like a slow but fiscally powerful wave out from the center of Manhattan, which lay forty miles to the east, the suburbs advanced a mile or two each year into the hills and fields and remaining wooded wilderness of New Jersey, so that in the sixteen years since the Brays had gotten married the population of Waynesboro had quadrupled. Farm after farm had been annexed into the maze of winding suburban avenues, corporations had moved research centers and even their headquarters

out into the "country," as they called it, and this of
course brought the bank where Mr. Bray worked (which
had been a little local concern to start with) a booming
business, which led to expansion and, for the employees,
unlooked-for professional opportunities. Mr. Bray soon
found himself, simply by virtue of being young, white,
and male, managing one of the new branches of the
bank, located in a pretty, "rustic" red-brick building
with big glass windows, built in one of the villages
which until five years ago had boasted only a church, a
general store, and a service station, and now had real-
estate and doctors' offices, a supermarket, and even a
small restaurant lined up along its single main street.

In their purchase of a home the Brays had been particularly lucky. After two years in the garage apartment,
they'd made a bid on a small, two-bedroom house in the
center of Waynesboro. With a loan from their parents,
they were able to make the down-payment on it, and
with Mr. Bray's advancement at the bank they were
soon having no trouble meeting mortgage payments on
a regular basis. After the twins were in school, Mrs.
Bray went to work as a receptionist at one of the first
unisex hairdressers to open in Waynesboro, so that they
were, as a family, kept busy and financially sound. Still,
they were mindful that in the years since they had
bought their house real-estate prices had at the very
least trebled, bringing an increasing property-tax burden
and making it clear that, whatever stroke of luck had
allowed them to settle in a community where Mrs. Bray
had grown up and only ten miles away from where Mr.
Bray had gone to school, the twins would very likely not
ever be able to afford to live in the town where they were
raised. It was growing too rich and too exclusive, and
even if they'd had the money to stay there it was not the

same place anymore; it was not a place you ended up in naturally. It was a place you won your way into by a fight you had at least partially to believe in. But this was a thing which saddened the parents of the Brays more than it did the Brays themselves, and perhaps it wasn't important because the parents of the Brays were old, they didn't know what they were talking about (Mrs. Bray had never been so excited as when she'd helped open the unisex hairdresser), they'd soon be dead anyway, and the Bray twins didn't care where they lived as long as everything went their way.

But were the Brays in love? Had they ever felt their hearts go out entirely to someone—perhaps to each other or perhaps to a stranger met on the street or someone from long ago and far away who had long since moved off, the way everyone did these days, someone who was "successful" now?

The Brays had never been in love with anyone but each other ("I was never in love with anybody till I met your father," Mrs. Bray told her twins, making it sound like it might almost be someone other than Mr. Bray she was talking about), but when seen from the outside, the Brays' love seemed more like a mutual succumbing to propaganda than like the highest ideal of what love can be; it seemed very much like two empty mirrors reflecting someone else's dream back and forth to each other in a cosmetic rather than an integral interaction. This is not to say that they didn't believe in the propaganda they used, but their belief was the kind that has only to be memorized and stuck to—"I love Mrs. Bray," "I love Mr. Bray"—rather than ever thought out or felt through. It was a belief that skirted its way nervously around any hint of an ambiguity or a dynamic. The belief was like a small man in their heads which they had periodically to wind up and listen to. They followed his instructions and they tried hard not to listen to anything else, and this made them nervous and cautious in dealing with their friends, neighbors, and colleagues, in addition to making them behave inconsistently with their children and uncomfortably with each other.

Mrs. Bray was a small pert blonde who had been a cheerleader once and was, in many ways, a cheerleader still; and although his good looks had suffered quite a deterioration in recent years, Mr. Bray was still an attractive and, one realized with a chance physical contact (a hand laid lightly on a shoulder, say), a sensual man, but this did not make them any more comfortable in the bedroom than in any of the other rooms in their house. They were perhaps the victims of their generation, here, for any natural animal impulse toward free-wheeling lust was curbed and undermined by a considerable physical embarrassment, largely on Mr. Bray's part. He had to have the lights out, undress in the dark, and then go to his embrace full of shame, gather his wife in his arms, bend over her as though to protect her while doing this thing to her. Then they would fall asleep in a heap beneath the covers and she would seem so small, so tiny, in the dark, that he'd feel he had molested a child, but that it was all over now, and he was a child now, too, in his striped pajamas, under the covers, yes, he was the same as her . . . he was a child like she was — until it was impossible to connect himself with the man who had shut off the light, undressed, and let a voice that came from the earth (from beneath the floorboards, beneath the cement floor of the cellar, over to the left, not too far from the septic tank, to be precise) guide him he knew not where.

This perhaps explained the Brays' unswerving marital

fidelity, their disinclination to go to parties (Waynesboro
was by this time experiencing a near-euphoric plague of
divorces and separations), and Mr. Bray's gruffness (it
got more of a reaction out of him than anything else
they did) when he half-muttered, half-barked at the
twins, "Get some clothes on—for God's sake," as they
came out of the shower, stark naked, with towels slung
over their shoulders, and wandered into the kitchen,
ostensibly for an apple to eat on the way upstairs, but
more for a glance of parental, and particularly maternal,
approval. Mrs. Bray handed them both apples, smiled
and blinked, as though she weren't seeing anything at
all or as if she had caught sight of a rabbit in a very far
field but then was not much disappointed at losing
sight of it.

It had taken the Brays all the courage in the world to
seduce each other, and there was, frankly, no courage or
time or even imagination enough left over for them to
consider arranging further extramarital or incestuous
seductions.

But were the Brays in love, in love, *in Love?*

Love is an absurd thing to ask about in such strident
terms and it is only when you are not busy enough that
the question (it was Mrs. Bray who asked it, of no one in
particular, more often than did Mr. Bray, although he
was guilty of asking too; anyone else either didn't care
or was much too ready to answer the question with a
bitter and envious simplistic "Yes!") formulates itself in
just this way.

And the answer was: Within certain limited spheres
of habitual activity which constituted the mainstay of
their life together, the Brays had indeed grown used to
and learned to tolerate each other.

Mr. Bray was sulky. Mrs. Bray was wiry and delightful

and could get on your nerves. There was always tension but this could always be held at bay because they were neither of them masochists, they had no inclination to explore and elaborate upon anything that might be unpleasant. They counted the marriage a success—at least Mrs. Bray did. And she was the woman, she was the one responsible for evaluating such things. Mr. Bray would take her word for it if she told him it was so, although privately he might not necessarily have counted himself happy if some secret call had been made upon him to think about it. But there had been no such call, whether secret or overt. And besides, marital success and happiness (the idea of happiness, in Mr. Bray's mind, was almost synonymous with effortlessness and ease) were two different things, just as were career success and job satisfaction.

Mr. Bray was in some ways comfortable with Mrs. Bray and his family, but in other ways he was not comfortable with them at all. He didn't have anyone to drink with, so he hardly ever drank, because drinking with his wife just wasn't the same as drinking had been so long ago, it didn't trigger and release anything. All he ever drank now was beer, and not too much of it. And he didn't really enjoy these scout troop campouts; so much had to be organized, and really it was much more responsibility than he wanted to take on, especially when it was his own boys who cut up the worst and got the other boys started. It wasn't at all the same as camping had been before—quiet, remote. But he couldn't do that quiet type of camping anymore, because neither of the twins wanted to go with him (they made no secret of the fact that the presence of their father bored them infinitely) and his wife didn't want to go either (everything got so dirty, she said), and he really didn't want to go on his own.

So instead he spent Saturday and Sunday drinking beer slowly, sitting in his La-Z-Boy chair and watching football or basketball on television. He had never particularly cared for sports, but he had dedicated himself to picking up at least the basics of the requisite two or three so as to have something to talk about with Mr. Cantwell, the main bank manager, when he came to inspect. Mr. Cantwell would come and check procedures, talk a bit of finance, all of which Mr. Bray was able to handle competently and intelligently, and then, for a parting shot, would always say something along the lines of "Well, what did you think of the Raiders last night?" which was calculated to put Mr. Bray at ease but which instead thoroughly mortified him.

Mr. Cantwell had a long line of how-to-talk-to-anybody-about-anything books on his desk at home. Bray had been a hard nut to crack—not interested in cars, or sex (at least he wasn't interested in sizing up some of the tellers he had working for him), nor did he have any political interest that Mr. Cantwell could see. (Mr. Bray kept so quiet about Communists that, if this hadn't been a banking business, Mr. Cantwell would have suspected him of being one—and he still wasn't sure.) He wasn't interested in money really (he did his job well, but he made no investments of his own apart from a standard savings account, which other people invested for him), and he wasn't ambitious apparently (he seemed perfectly content to continue indefinitely as manager of this negligible branch of Waynesboro Bank & Trust). Furthermore, he had no interest in nuclear warfare (Mr. Cantwell kept close tabs on the arms race—the potential and perhaps imminent transformation of the Soviet Union into a feebly glowing wasteland of radioactive ash and dust worked like an inspiration, a highly moral and cleansing motivating force in his mind). Mr. Bray didn't even seem interested or impressed by the leaps and bounds with which Waynesboro was progressing and becoming at one with the modern age (Mr. Cantwell had been instrumental in changing Waynesboro's legal name from Waynesboro Township to the Waynesboro Incorporated Metropolitan Area, a change which had cost taxpayers an estimated seventy-five thousand dollars because of abstruse litigious procedures involved).

Sports, then, it must be sports.

So Mr. Bray and Mr. Cantwell both spent precious hours of their weekends watching a screen, Mr. Cantwell trying to think of "hooks" as he called them (this was a term found in one of his books—you used a hook, threw it to or at someone, and pulled, and then they *had* to answer you), while Mr. Bray tried to anticipate what comment Mr. Cantwell would have to make on Monday morning.

Drinking beer with the television on was not so bad; it was soothing. The Brays had a color television and the bright uniforms moved back and forth across the screen while the sports commentators gave Mr. Bray some idea of ways he could parry with Mr. Cantwell, if only he didn't lose his nerve when the time came, about what had gone on in the game.

Mr. Bray asked some of the slightly younger men at the bank to come watch football on a Sunday, but they either refused (always with deep appreciation of the offer) or came once, were bored, and never managed to come again.

Sometimes Mr. Bray would take his wife out for a meal

during a game, deliberately. They would eat and talk about the boys or about the food they were eating. Mr. Bray would keep them out until it was getting on time for the game to end, and then they'd go back home to catch the score (even if you miss the game, you have to catch the score). This way on Monday he could be the one who opened the conversation: "Couldn't catch the game, had to take the wife out to eat, you know how it is, but I heard the Raiders won."

Mr. Cantwell picked up on this, at first, as a foray into the marital-gripe vein, a vein which was, frankly, far more interesting and even more useful to him than were sports, but all further probing proved unavailing to him. Mr. Bray was happily married and that was how he would stay.

What Mr. Cantwell didn't know and what he didn't have the means to find out (being one of the most intimidating figures in Mr. Bray's far-from-encouraging pantheon) was that Mr. Bray was uncomfortable in his dealings with almost everyone, even the female secretaries and tellers at the bank, who were all as fond of Mr. Bray as they could be—he was so shy! Of course he had his off-days and sometimes some of them began to think he was a bit creepy, but this feeling was periodically dispelled whenever his wife came into the office and charmed them all with the mysterious way in which she somehow made Mr. Bray seem "more of a man." The two of them were (all the girls in the office agreed) "just right" for each other. Mr. Bray was the nicest man they had ever worked for, and on good days, when everything was going well, they sang his praises and placed him high on a pedestal, with an adulation which embarrassed him ("Oh, Mr. Bray—you're so sweet!") because of the attention it drew and also, oddly, because in his eyes they *were* all beautiful (just as Mr. Cantwell said) and—a point which Mr. Cantwell tended to overlook—*nice* (except on their bad days, when they could be positively grim). And yet he didn't feel any desire for them the way some of them almost seemed to want him to feel; all he wanted was to just be friends, real friends. He didn't feel comfortable with any of them, they were too quick to respond, and when he thought back, and searched the past for a feeling of social relaxation, understanding, and pleasure, the only person he could think of was Bill Jewitt. Bill Jewitt was the only person with whom Mr. Bray had really ever felt reasonably at ease, and even then he had felt somewhat overawed by him. But in an odd way he sensed that Bill Jewitt had put trust in him, had taken him on as someone worth further pursuing, not for any particular end, social, romantic, or professional, but for the sake of something which, looking at it through time as though at a jewel gleaming at the far end of a very long penumbrous and ill-defined tunnel, Mr. Bray could only call "freedom" or, perhaps (since in the United States "freedom" has a slightly shrill and jingoistic political connotation), something called "life."

What had happened to Bill Jewitt? What had that friendship consisted of?

It was one of those typical school friendships in which, without much being said, certainly without any questions being asked, on a kind of immediate intuitive impulse, total rapport and acceptance are at once established. Bill Jewitt was older than Mr. Bray by about six months, but this difference of age was made to seem greater than it was by Bill's greater experience of the world, especially in the realm of alcohol. Also, Bill Jewitt was in many ways more physical than Mr. Bray—he seemed to eat, sleep, talk, and exert himself physically more than Mr.

Bray, who was tall but with an airy build, soft-spoken, not a sound sleeper, and not in the habit of eating much. Bill Jewitt could as easily have chosen to persecute Mr. Bray as to take him under his wing, and there was an element in the friendship which never allowed Mr. Bray to forget this. In an unspoken way Bill Jewitt entirely set the terms, but as Mr. Bray could never have come up with terms of his own, this felt more like being made an accomplice rather than like being led or dominated.

In terms of women, Mr. Bray had been an asset to Bill Jewitt because he was so popular and added a softer edge to Bill Jewitt's somewhat rough image. His affiliation with Bill Jewitt, in turn, put Mr. Bray on a more advantageous footing with the rest of the boys. These comments might imply that there was a strategy between them, but there was not—there was no conversation, no recognition of each other, beyond the very basics. The friendship had started with Bill Jewitt approaching Mr. Bray in a high school corridor one day and proposing out of the blue: "You wanna go camping?" Mr. Bray had answered partly out of fear and partly out of a pleasure which he tried to restrain, "Yes." He, Mr. Bray, supplied the tent; Bill Jewitt supplied the beer and, later on, on rare occasions, whiskey. Their entire conversation over this idyll of a year or two, culminating in that last summer, consisted of "You got any money?" "You wanna get some beer?" "You drunk yet?" "I gotta take a piss." "I gotta take a shit." "When you gotta be home?" "I think I'm gonna be sick," and "Shit, I think it's gonna rain."

After the summer between their senior year in high school and the fall when Mr. Bray went away to college (that summer seemed an eternity, a center of time, like the friendship itself, a main light by which Mr. Bray saw everything that had gone before and everything that came after), Bill Jewitt had joined the army, gone away to Nevada, and then come back after two years, just when Mr. Bray was deciding to get married. But Bill Jewitt didn't come back on his own feet. He had been in a helicopter crash, not in any combat zone but while in training, and broken both his legs. They had sent him to a veterans' hospital near Waynesboro, because aside from the fractures there had been nerve damage and he would need extensive physical therapy in order to learn to walk again; the therapy would take at least a year, it was estimated, and so Bill, being apprised of this, had put in a request to be near his family and friends. By "family and friends" he had mostly meant Mr. Bray, almost as though it were his son he was wanting to see. He conveyed this wish to his parents on arrival at the VA and they contacted the Brays, who in turn contacted their son at college. The two sets of parents, who, until their sons had met, had not known each other, now constituted the only channel through which communications between Mr. Bray and Bill Jewitt were made because, as a natural consequence of the way they had both been brought up, it had never occurred to them that two men could write letters to each other. In their families, it had been the women who knew how to write and what to say.

Mr. Bray went to see Bill Jewitt at the hospital in early June on a sunlit day which was not yet too hot or oppressive with the full heavy heat of a Jersey summer. From the road, the institution looked like a parody of a red-brick colonial mansion, several stories high, with a tower with a sun cupola in the middle and enormous wings off to the side with smokestacks rising from them. Although all in proportion with itself, it had the odd unreality of things that are too big for the landscape in which they appear. At a distance of about a mile from the hospital buildings, in all directions, there was a tall wire fence, topped with barbed wire and broken up by only a few carefully guarded entrances. Between the fence and the buildings lay a golf course for the patients, a lake, and small patches of woods. It was like the setting for a dream. Lost souls wandered slowly and aimlessly as though through Elysian fields from which they would never escape.

Inside the building, yellow electric light reflected off not-quite-white tile walls and floors; a mixed crew of nurses, doctors, nurses' aides (frightened or cheerful fifteen- and sixteen-year-olds), secretaries, and patients wandered at large in the corridors. The corridors went on forever and Mr. Bray had to ask directions three times and assure two doctors and a nurse that he was not a patient himself before he could find his friend. When he finally did find him, he was sitting in a common room with a number of other men, playing a game of cards, sitting in a wheelchair with a blanket draped over his shattered legs. Bill Jewitt was immensely glad to see him but the meeting was awkward because of all the other people there and also because Mr. Bray didn't know what to say. First he said, "Do you want to go for a walk somewhere?" and Bill Jewitt pointed to the wheels of the wheelchair, saying that if they wanted to go to the canteen they'd have to use the elevator and he wasn't sure that visitors were allowed to use the elevator, they had funny rules here. The strange way this was said and the unusual and unprecedented deference to rules it implied (Bill Jewitt had never cared about rules before in his life) made Mr. Bray feel he had come farther from home than he had ever previously been, almost as if he had come to a strange and distant foreign country where all the physical laws to which he was normally subject had been reversed (here he was, walking—while Bill Jewitt apparently could not even stand up), and this so upset him that he announced much sooner than he had originally envisaged announcing it that he would be getting married soon. He announced this almost in shame, as though it were a betrayal of some kind, and at the same time almost in defense against something he could not ever possibly have named.

But, if he thought this sudden catapulted announcement of a marriage might put things on a more stable ground between them, he could not have been more unnerved by Bill Jewitt's strange reply and also by the strange undirected look in his eyes, which seemed to take Mr. Bray into account but only in the context of half a million other things: "Aw, that's good 'cause otherwise me and you could maybe get an apartment together and not have to pay so much rent."

Mr. Bray didn't know what to say to this.

But he didn't have to say anything, because just at that moment a nurse came in and gave Bill Jewitt his medication "before the rest of the boys," so he wouldn't have to wait in line in his wheelchair at the medication station at three o'clock.

Then the conversation proceeded a little more normally. Bill Jewitt asked Mr. Bray what his future wife was like and Mr. Bray tried hard to describe her but he found that he'd never really thought consciously about her before, not enough to remember anything about her apart from some jewelry she had that she'd made him look at, but he didn't think Bill Jewitt would be interested in this beyond the comment "She wears nice jewelry."

Bill Jewitt said, "Well, I'd sure like to be your best

man except I never heard of a best man in a wheelchair before."

To which Mr. Bray replied, "Well, I don't know . . ." and stared at Bill Jewitt because he, Mr. Bray, hadn't even thought about a best man yet, there being no date set for the wedding, what with parental disapproval still looming large on the horizon, so he added, "Neither of our parents want us to do it yet."

And in turn Bill Jewitt said, "I'm the only guy in here who has something like this," he nodded to his legs, "who wasn't in a war. I'm the only guy in here who has something like this because of a dumb accident," as though he had only himself to blame, like the difference between getting drunk on his own and getting drunk at a party.

And then it was time for Mr. Bray to go.

He never went back to see Bill Jewitt again, although the VA hospital was only fifteen miles away from his parents' house.

Bill Jewitt stayed at that VA for a year, until he could walk. Then he was sent out of state to a place where he could get military-funded vocational training. Just recently, Mr. Bray had heard, Bill Jewitt had come back to New Jersey and, after eighteen years, was in the VA once more—this time with leukemia. There was beginning to be a minor scandal. Bill Jewitt had been among the men sent into radioactive areas just hours after detonation in the series of above-ground tests in Nevada during the fifties. He probably didn't have long to live; there was only so much the doctors could do at this point and then the game was up. But, even though there was so little time and even though the hospital was closer than ever (only three miles away from the branch of the bank which Mr. Bray now managed), Mr. Bray somehow could not muster the courage it seemed to take to go and see him.

Aside from Bill Jewitt, Mr. Bray had no friends. He had met a few of his wife's friends' husbands, and they seemed nice, but whenever he'd been introduced and then left alone with one of them at a party, the two men always found they had nothing to say to each other. Long ago, he'd exchanged one or two Christmas cards with some old college acquaintances whose pranks or escapades he might still occasionally talk about with his wife, but he'd long since let the effort of communication with them fold and go under. Perhaps he had real need of friends, perhaps a vital part of him (the part that everyone had liked, had found attractive in high school and in college) would sink out of sight without access to any easygoing, natural, nonromantic contact, leaving him with a gap which might consume him, shut him away forever from a way which, if he were to be told it was possible and given directions as to how it might be had, he would like to be.

But he was like a sleeper who is chilly in his dream and does not know to reach out, in his sleep, and pull the fallen blanket back over his body, over his shoulders.

"Over there—over where those bumps are's where we're gonna be camping." Mr. Gough's bulbous head vaguely indicated a direction off to the side of the dirt road they were following.

To the left and to the right was a holly forest, apparently natural; Mr. Davies had never seen anything like it before. The trees were low and twisted, with leaves that were pointed and waxy green, painful to push your way into, he imagined. In fact, these thickets must be impenetrable. They grew no more than ten feet high and yet had the proportions and aged look of normal trees, so that they seemed to present a forest in miniature. He would have to write home to his father about it—this was the kind of thing that interested him.

Chris Castle was interested in the holly forest too but, unlike his stepfather, he didn't think it was impenetrable. A thick screen of foliage grew at its outer edges, but inside there was a clear space, about four or five feet high, where birds and perhaps squirrels scurried and flew, below a canopy of leaves so dense that even on the brightest days the light in there was a deep, penumbral, aquatic green—on days with clouds it was closet-dark.

The tops of the trees gave no hint of their individuality but were one substance, billowing, rising, and falling in the shape of a wave, like a head of hair which the wind and ocean had swept just so, in a style that seemed a movement stopped in mid-air. And, just above that wave, in the direction which Mr. Gough's head indicated, were peculiar, symmetrical, evenly spaced sand dunes—an inexplicable and curious sight. For one thing they seemed much too big, they seemed out of all proportion to the rest of this little hook of land projecting into the entrance of a bay. And, for another, if the small scale of the holly forest seemed a slightly surreal caprice of Nature, the even spacing and identical shaping of these dunes seemed beyond caprice—more a perversity or sickness.

Something was obviously up. Mr. Gough violently nodded his head two or three times toward the campground, saying with a strange pride in his grumbly voice, which both Mr. Davies and Chris had trouble under-standing, "Over there—over where those bumps are—over there." He pronounced "bumps" almost as though it might be two syllables, and his insistence on the word couldn't help but sound slightly addled.

About half a mile farther down the dirt road, they came to a sign pointing down a smaller track to the left which proclaimed in jubilant multicolored letters: JAMBOREEEEE! The track in itself, on another occasion, would have seemed somber, desolate-looking, cutting narrowly through the thick groves of holly, but what with the colorful sign and the sight of older scouts and scoutmasters and other men in even more official-looking military uniforms wandering up and down it now, it was obviously a way toward the most serious kind of festivities.

And, indeed, the track led through to an open sandy field, where swarms of scouts and scoutmasters, all in their green uniforms, were either working together (setting up latrines, directing trucks which had brought water in cooling tanks on back, putting up tents) or fooling around, watching the others work.

An Explorer scout was standing at the entrance to the field, directing the incoming traffic. He pointed out which direction they should follow after Mr. Gough barked out their troop number (there was nothing Mr. Gough liked better than giving official information). To his directions, the Explorer added the warning to "keep between the flagged markers, sir—or we'll have to dig you out of the sand," and then he waved them on, turning his attention to the next car. Up and down the field, designated paths of traffic had been marked by sticks with bright red strips of rag tied around them at the top—a red, almost vermilion, which shone out, in contrast with the drab green of the field and men, like tense and fluttering rows of flame of unknown origin. Casually glanced at, from a certain distance, they could not be correlated with the paths they marked, but seemed to hover and create a pattern that was altogether superimposed, self-contained, and removed from the landscape.

In addition to the flagged markers, there were big two-by-fours stuck in the soft ground, with troop numbers written on white placards nailed at the top. Mr. Gough drove on, the station wagon bumping and creaking along this improvised road, until they came to a placard which said in big numerals "431"—whereupon they pulled over to one side, slipping between markers, stopped, got out of the car, and looked around.

The first thing they noticed was the change in the air—the change from the air inside the air-conditioned car, of course, but more important, the change from the last fresh air they had breathed in Waynesboro to the fresh air they were breathing here. The air in Waynesboro tasted of leaves and lawns. Here, however, all the air was salt ocean, with the bay on one side and the open sea on the other. The holly might add a muskiness to the smell, but even it was mostly there because it could tolerate this salt. And the grasses were salt sea grasses. The sky here was more capricious, anything could blow off the ocean, and (they all looked up) seagulls turned and cried in this different sky.

When they all looked back down again, they saw Mr. Wing's car pulling up alongside Mr. Gough's, bringing Jim Gough, the Berringer brothers, Danny McDaniels, and two of the younger boys to join the crowd.

Mr. Gough walked up and addressed Mr. Wing where he sat in the driver's seat.

"Seen Bray?"

Mr. Wing smiled. "No, we lost him."

Mr. Gough laughed as though there could not be better news than this. Then he started giving orders: "Okay, unload the cars, put the tents over there, that's right, keep the food in the back of the station wagon, hey's that your pack, McDaniels? it's comin' undone, Clay, help him with his pack will ya?—that's it." He turned to his son, Jim, and said, "Take these and take one of the boys and see if you can get some water—looks like they got some over there."

Jim Gough chose Roger Bray to help him fetch the water, a choice which Mr. Gough hadn't thought quickly enough to try to prevent and which he couldn't really reverse now because, after all, it made some sense—water was heavy, especially in those big ten-gallon containers which the troop used, and, after Jim, the Bray twins were the strongest of the boys in the troop. Still, he threw a look of disgust after them, as he would have after any seditionary forces going out into the world, as soon as their backs were turned. And there was something in their gait, it could not be denied, that made it obvious that they were considering how so simple a task as fetching water could be turned into the sort of fiasco that could give a moment's outrageous pleasure.

"Clay, go stand by that turnoff of the road down there and see if you can catch Mr. Bray when he comes along, eh?"

"I'm helping McDaniels with his pack, sir."

"Blue, you go do it then."

Blue Berringer went with speed and without a word, remembering that his father was in that car and might stay permanently lost if some effort wasn't made to retrieve him.

Mr. Gough watched Blue take off and then, standing with tent poles in his hand which he shook as he spoke, he said, "Goddamn Bray'd drive right off the goddamn Hook into the bay if someone didn't stop him." He dropped the poles down on the ground then and, as if this followed, turned to look in the direction of the water truck. He could see the truck all right and a line of scouts waiting to get water from it, but he couldn't see any sign of his son or the accompanying Bray twin (whichever twin it was — Mr. Gough couldn't tell them apart, although almost everyone else in the troop could) anywhere. They'd managed, within a minute, to disappear without a trace. Maybe there was a line on the other side of the truck too or maybe they'd stopped in the latrines or in the woods along the way (this was in fact the case) to take a leak after the long ride in the car. At any rate, this disappearance, which a few moments ago might have driven Mr. Gough to a point of fury, somehow bounced off him (Bray's customary lagging behind added zest to his spirits, too) and led him to address Mr. Davies, who had so far stood idle wondering what he could do, and Chris, his stepson, who was about to wander off, and say, "Well, whaddya thinka those bunkers, then?," jerking his head in their direction. And the meaning of the word came clear.

On Sandy Hook there are bunkers eighty feet high, one hundred yards long, and thirty yards across, standing at intervals of about two or three hundred yards along the Raritan Bay side of the narrow strip of land. To the east, they look out over the holly forest to the Atlantic Ocean and, to the north, on a clear day, you can get a fabulous view of lower New York Bay from the top of one of them. They were built during the Second World War, with what exact military purpose in mind no one can say, beyond the vague intention of guarding the southernmost entrance to New York Bay against the rampaging Germans. As the rampaging Germans never made it this far, apart from one or two prowling U-boats, the bunkers were never used. They have never been torn down either, although they will certainly be obsolete in whatever next crisis, military or otherwise, faces us. Inside them are dank concrete corridors with occasional ventilation shafts which pierce right through to the top and let down a dimming well of light. On their outside there is grass and shrubbery disguising them as "dunes," although they aren't like any other dunes to be found along this coast. They are vaguely portentous and vaguely absurd and so provide the perfect recreation ground for boys between the ages of eleven and sixteen. Already boys from different troops attending this jamboree were clambering up their sides, running along and shouting down from their tops. The air up there was alive, was cooler and more invigorating than the air down in the field, and it sent them spinning. Gulls were up there too, everything could be seen, and all that anyone would want in the world, if they could only have had the wish granted, was to walk on air even higher.

Mr. Davies and his stepson, Chris, and the rest of the boys and men connected with Troop 431 didn't look in the direction of the bunkers for very long, however, for here came Mr. Bray, with Mr. Berringer, Anthony Wing, Billy Bray, and Chuckie Massie in the car with him — arriving only ten minutes after the first two vehicles of the convoy had gotten here. Jim Gough and Roger Bray came back with huge containers of water, which they set down by the cars with a grunt and a show of strength. Blue Berringer came sprinting back from the spot where he'd stood guard with the Explorer scout and found Mr. Bray; it seemed to him this ought to be his moment. But apparently it wasn't. Too much energy was being released with the Bray twins being together and fooling around already, with Jim Gough leaning quiet against Mr. Bray's car, grinding the heel of a muddy, sandy boot against Mr. Bray's car's shiny fender (which Mr. Bray didn't like, but didn't have the courage to protest), looking on at the twins, possessive and proud, as though he owned them, as though they were his. Blue Berringer remained in the background, irretrievably on the fringe of things, thinking that perhaps if Mr. Bray had been a little more lost, perhaps if he, Blue, had had to go to a slightly more out-of-the-way place to discover him — say, Asbury Park — then! But he was able to take his meditation no further. Mr. Gough cut short the Brays' horseplay in his usual bellicose style, everything was reorganized, order was restored in the ranks, tents were extracted from the car trunk and the backs of the station wagons, and work on the campsite was begun, so that Blue Berringer had to pay attention.

Here, in fact, the Berringer boys and Mark Wing came into their own—improvising tent pegs where the real thing was missing, making sure the tent fronts were in a perfectly straight line and that the fly lines didn't extend from the tents too far, chucking away rocks and stones, and checking for the most even pieces of ground were all things these three managed to do well. Even Jim Gough lent his assistance—particularly with knots: a bowline, two half-hitches. Of the men connected with the troop, it was Mr. Berringer whom Jim Gough held in the greatest respect, and this had led to Jim's making knots his area of expertise. In addition to the usual scout repertoire, he too made endless hangman's nooses and more idio-syncratic knots of his own invention, the unifying characteristic of which was their complete disintegration at the slightest tug upon a certain salient but far from obvious loop or loose end, knots which brute force (Jim Gough enjoyed challenging his father) only pulled tighter. Tents that Jim Gough worked on inevitably had more knots than were necessary, especially on their fly lines, but rarely more than were tasteful or attractive. Curlicues of rope gave Jim's tents the dignity, almost, of Celtic or Anglo-Saxon decorative stonework.

The boys' tents were all pup tents and relatively easy to set up, whereas the men's tent was difficult; it was a luxury stand-up tent, with a fly and an open vestibule, where everybody huddled on campouts when it rained, and then a tent-within-a-tent for cozy sleeping. On this trip, it was more than filled to capacity, as it officially slept only four.

The process of setting up the men's tent was arduous

and complicated. First, the tent frame had to be constructed. With repeated camping trips, the pieces of the frame had been bent and so were awkward to fit together, each pole now having to fit a specific corner of the roof frame, whereas before they'd all been interchangeable, so that the tent was like a thing accumulating secrets as it went along. Next, the inner tent had to be hung from the frame, where it would look fragile and naked like a shower curtain from behind which one half expected a brown body to emerge. Its walls were made of netting, which rippled and let light and shapes come through as though it were the ghost of a tent. And finally the outer wall of the tent was slung over, pulled down tight on the frame, and pegged, every six inches or so, to the earth. With Jim Gough's assistance, they had all this done in ten minutes' time. And, when the tent stood there complete, and the men, by accident, found themselves standing one at each corner of it, with Mr. Davies standing to one side a little, it appeared as if there was nothing that could ever deny or fail to attribute to them the hallmark of grownup competence and authority.

The Bray twins were certainly trying to make inroads on this authority, however, with the tentative appearances of their tent (a slightly bigger than usual pup tent which they would share with Jim Gough tonight) first here, then there, followed by Mr. Gough's "Goddamnit, no!" which, successively, forbade them (1) to set up their tent as far as possible from the men's tent, with its back to the rest of the boys' tents and at an unusual but attractive thirty-five-degree angle to the perfectly straight line in which Blue Berringer had had these tents arranged; (2) to set up their tent in a small clearing just inside the holly grove ("Goddamnit no! Not under the goddamn trees!") fifty yards away; (3) to set up their tent, in a strategical dare, so close to the men's tent that they would be able to use the same tent pegs along one side; (4) to set up their tent in the perfectly straight line Blue Berringer had created, only with their entrance facing the opposite way from that of their neighbors.

The final compromise was that their tent remained the one farthest removed from the men's tent, but in a straight line with the rest of the boys' tents and with its entrance facing the same way as theirs, too. This was satisfying to the men, or at least to Mr. Gough and Mr. Bray (Mr. Davies and Mr. Berringer didn't know enough to care one way or the other—and Mr. Wing didn't count in matters like this)—to Mr. Gough because, in an interesting attempt to turn the tables on the twins and his son with an inversion of a certain natural order (assuming that one saw that order as reaching its acme of perfection with the inhabitants of the men's tent and tapering out toward atavistic chaos along the little line of tents which ended with the Bray twins' and Jim Gough's), he delegated some authority to his son and the twins, telling them to keep an eye on the younger boys in the tent next to theirs, deeming that tonight it would be better to have these three terrorizing the younger members of their own troop than, at one or two in the morning, to have them wandering the jamboree at large. And indeed this was a cunningly calculated distraction —interfering with the younger boys' late-night business (which would inevitably be going on) might well be enough to keep Jim and the twins within relative bounds.

Mr. Gough had a good instinct when it came to strategical vying with the enemy; he knew enough to tackle them on their own terms, his ultimate coup having been on a camping trip in the early spring when it was still chilly. The three boys had taken off at about two in the morning with a fair amount of whispering and scuffling that had wakened Mr. Gough. He'd waited until they were gone and then crept into their tent and hidden their sleeping bags. This done, he'd gone back to sleep. Between cold (they searched all the cars, everyone's tent, the latrines, everywhere, but they never thought to look for their sleeping bags in the place where Mr. Gough had hidden them: in their own packs in their own tents), sleeplessness, and some beer they'd bought at a nearby 7-11, they'd barely made it through to the Sunday. They'd had to concede Mr. Gough's victory, for it was exactly the kind of victory they could respect; he'd managed to fool them in a way they approved of, but there was an element of escalation in this ongoing game of do-we? dare-we? and it seemed as though a breaking point would soon be reached. This jamboree might be the final testing ground before Jim and the twins dropped out of the scouts for good, for it was obvious they weren't interested in going on with it much longer.

Mr. Bray, for his part, was satisfied with the arrangements of the tents because of a delusion that the farther off his twins were (earshot marking the boundaries of total absolution) the less they were his responsibility—this delusion stemming from the, to his mind, unarguable premise that a man like him couldn't possibly be expected to keep up with boys like those.

No sooner had all the tents been set up and the equipment taken out of the cars than Mr. Gough blew the whistle he had hanging around his neck and, thus commanding some attention, ordered everyone to eat lunch. They all got out their packed lunches and ate them. And no sooner had the lunches been eaten than Mr. Gough blew his whistle again and called for a uniform inspection. All the boys had to line up while

Mr. Gough and Mr. Wing examined them one by one and evaluated their personal appearance: "McDaniels, you got two buttons still missin' from your shirt, didn't I tell ya get your motherta sew 'em back on?" "Yes, sir." "Well, what seems to be the problem, then?" "Soon as I get home, sir." "That's not good enough." "I'm sorry, sir." Mr. Wing, who was big on the correct placement of insignia, asked Blue Berringer if it wasn't more in line to stick his three-year pin on the actual flap of his left front pocket rather than above the flap, to which Blue replied, "I don't think so, sir, but I'll be glad to check up on it."

Then, following on from the uniform inspection, came marching.

Mr. Gough drilled them, he marched them up and down, he marched them over the road and back across the road. He made them halt and come to a standstill with a rhythmic stamping of first the left foot, then the right foot. And then he started them back up again. Mr. Wing, whose impulse it was always to elaborate on whatever was at hand, had them try fanning out and marching in a circle, with one boy (Chris Castle) marching at the center (and getting dizzy turning round and round) while the twins and Jim Gough marched at the outer rim, faster and faster, in comical strides, until Jim Gough broke into a goosestep sprint much faster than any of the younger boys could keep up with. The circle's diameter wavered, stretched, collided with the tents—and completely disintegrated.

"Maybe that wasn't such a good idea" was all Mr. Wing had to offer, while boys giggled and Mr. Gough, shouting, "Fall in! Fall in, goddamnit!," took charge and restored order to the ranks once more. They marched on. They marched to the edge of the holly grove and then, "Abououou . . . t—*face!*"—they marched back to the tents again. They marched in standing position. The sun was hot and it felt like the whole landscape was marching, succumbing to a series of constant rhythmic jolts. Mr. Wing had another idea and wanted them to march in a figure eight, but this was vetoed by Mr. Gough: "For cryin' out loud, whaddya think this is—a goddamn skatin' rink?"

They marched for half an hour and attracted the attention of some gulls and even of a few crows. Mr. Gough bellowed out directions and his voice was regular and gruff, like the waves. Gulls hovered and glided, made trajectories, gave their cries, and then moved off to a distance, to study this spectacle in its entirety. The crows roosted in the holly trees and, after the troop approached and marched away from these, flapped to the ground and searched as if for food. When a bird dropping just missed the head and, in fact, the eye of McDaniels and landed, instead, on his left boot, he didn't say a word, although what with the sun and birds and the drumming march he was about to pass out or vomit, but just marched on.

Then the marching stopped.

Mr. Gough turned and surveyed the great campgrounds, as if to see what effect such discipline and order as that of his troop had had upon the world. And it was something invisible in the air which answered him, which let him see what he wanted to see, so that he was appeased but not entirely satisfied. The salt in the air was a disturbing element; it didn't promise anything. If he could have made the association, if he could have connected a memory, salt with salt, he would have realized he was thinking of his year in the Pacific, stationed on one island base and then another, but never seeing any action. His military experience had amounted to an island holiday, only with men and no women and with beaches all to yourself, followed by over a quarter of a century of passionate absorption in war books, documentaries, government-authorized footage, encyclopedias of aircraft, war vessels, tanks, guns, armaments, and uniforms of every kind, until his own "war year" was almost eclipsed, could not be distinguished from a dream anymore. He might have recalled the boredom, the discomfort of waiting, or, more to the point, the contempt in the look that some of the soldiers coming back from "action" had given the troops that sat on a quiet island, an island dream, with thunder in the background, waiting to get on with it and find out what "it" was all about. But, even had he remembered this, it would not have been for Mr. Gough to decipher the utter dispiritedness, the damaging defeat in some of these men's faces at the uncovered violence and simplicity in themselves, traits which, under a banner of glory, hadn't been the ones they'd expected to be uncovered.

Instead he looked into the air and he was like a squirrel or a cat or a hog, vacantly staring, unconsciously thinking of its natural function, while trucks and cars and boys passed back and forth across his field of vision in paths much less symmetrical and much more like the elaborate and restricting trails which ants, in their freedom, invent for themselves than Mr. Gough could ever imagine. What he saw instead was another, simpler order—and what this order did was create a small resting pillow, but also, strangely, a harassing impatience at the back of his brain.

It was Mr. Davies, ultimately, who drew his attention to the general call that was being made all around them.

From speakers lashed to the top of a tall pole in the center of the campground came a distorted voice announcing the events and competitions of the afternoon, in which all troops were expected to take part. The voice echoed and stretched and rasped and fell flat. To have such a voice in a place such as this, with open air and sky curved over a huge garden of sea grasses and sand, was like having two songs sung at once, but at the moment the song of the voice was stronger, and troops of green began to draw from all corners of the sprawling campsite toward a central location. Mr. Gough got his troop assembled and they began to walk, silent, in Indian file, toward the blare of the speaker. Only Mr. Berringer stayed behind. He had an idea; he'd had it just before he'd left Waynesboro.

The ground in the mountains is so hard, so full of flint. Thousands of years ago glaciers came and then retreated, leaving moraines. Trees twist their roots around these and make it impossible to dig.

But here the ground was soft, soft as could be. Out of his pack he extracted a little folding shovel, usually used for digging latrines. He unfolded it, set to work. This was an experiment. In his mind he had a picture of a Dutch oven, of how big it was and how it would fit in a hole in the ground. In the mountains he'd tried this but the ground wouldn't give—you'd need a pickax or a crowbar to pry away boulders. It was easier heating stones, piling them on top; it was hard getting inside the ground to get at stones to try to heat them. Pity the poor people trying to bury their dead! At the back of his eyes, which was where he saw himself, he felt a closeness to the stones and twisted roots, he felt an affinity; this sand was a thing he had no respect for, but in it his experiment might work. Get a big hole, line it with coals, put in the oven—it would be easier to cover and heat from all sides if it was already almost buried. He knew a way of cooking applesauce and gingerbread batter together, in alternating layers, if the heat was even. The gingerbread came out moist, the applesauce was better than cream—a real treat if it worked, another trick all his own.

The sand turned fine and dirty, came in layers, as he dug down deep. After nine inches it was almost powdered mud, dust which rose at the bite and scrape of the shovel. It had been dry this summer and this soil dried out quicker than any other. He got down on his knees, rounded the hole, made its edges neat. Troops filed past. He dug and dug till he couldn't have been dirtier. His face and hands and sleeves and knees were blanketed in grayish dust, making his eyes the only bright thing that looked out from him. His hair was filled with it. He dug this hole in front of the men's tent, not very far from the road, so that all who went past got a look at him. And, as he became aware of how dirty he was getting, he plunged in deeper, not caring anymore. The voice of the speaker he ignored: . . . *has supplied us with portable latrines so please refrain from digging any holes in the campsite. . . .*

The last stragglers from the farthest end of the jamboree were coming by, heading for the voice which carried on with its solemn advice and calm warnings: . . . *would like to leave our park the way we found it. . . .*

Three younger boys with insignia which said "Dover, N.J." and a troop number sewn on their sleeves hurried by, trying to get their caps straight and their neckerchiefs tied correctly as they went along. Mr. Berringer looked up, saw them coming, called out to them, "*Hey!*"

His was a voice of authority, however casual its format might be.

They all froze, turned, waited to hear what he'd say.

"Have you ever *seen* anyone so dirty?" he asked them. "Have you ever *seen* a man as dirty as me?" He held up his hands.

They almost sang—a deep low, "*No*-ooo . . . ooo . . . "

With that he broke into a smile like a satyr's.

They stared back at him, eyes opened wide in astonishment. No answer.

Then one of them cried out, "Crazy man!"—made the smile collapse . . . and they ran on off.

A flag that was not the stars and stripes was raised up into the air, into the sky. Whether it had a specific meaning which it presumed to impose on this jamboree or whether it had been invented especially for the purpose, no clue was given.

One thing, though, it did seem to indicate: that there were "games," "events" going on, being taken part in.

Hundreds of men and boys in uniform-green moved in a shifting swell, between points of concentration, up and down, up and down. Megaphoned voices carried on with nonstop announcements—they broadcast the name, and again the name, of some particular person who was asked to "please report to the emergency tent,—please report to the emergency tent." A brassy hilarious sound came on top of all this, on top of sounds of motors and cries. Looking over to the entrance to this field, to the narrow track which cut through the holly grove, where the brassy sound was coming from, Mr. Davies saw a military band shimmering in the heat and playing John Philip Sousa marches. The cymbals put a cutting edge on rhythms that were being swallowed and distorted by the wind. The big bass drum came through strong and then vanished, absorbed by the trees.

Mr. Davies closed his eyes—pictured this place devoid

of people, utterly silent; he imagined the hollow rustle a breeze would give through the unyielding surface of holly leaves, like the slightest insubstantial whistling under one's breath, through one's teeth. He put out his hand to where he thought Chris might be, and imagined himself following. And the sound seemed to cloud, to fog over, as though there were a tide that could make things which were near seem far away. He sank for a moment, in a trance, into a silence even deeper than this. *Imagine this whole continent abandoned, deserted —perhaps a bird or two left, drifting.*

Then the bass drum came back with a vengeance. The cymbals and a gull above his head made their sharp cries, as the wind swung round. He opened his eyes. Chris wasn't in sight.

Ian Davies stood still and realized that they hadn't made it even halfway here in the car before he'd begun to tell himself he wouldn't ever bother coming on one of these affairs again. Now that he was here, he was bored with and unreceptive to the events and the behavior of the people around him. It wasn't as though (as Laura had suggested it might be) this kind of thing brought him and Chris closer together—he'd lost track of Chris. And, even when he'd had Chris in sight, once they were out of the car Chris had appeared to be more oblivious of his stepfather's presence than Ian had ever known him to be (it didn't occur to him to notice that Chris was no more oblivious than any of the rest of the boys were of their fathers). But he wondered if, with the best intentions in the world, he would have trouble making this sound convincing to Laura, whose worries about Chris, after their living in Waynesboro for almost a year and his appearing to have made no friends, were on the rise and, in fact, getting to be a source of tension, occasionally, between her and Ian.

The move back to Waynesboro hadn't quite turned out as either of them had envisaged it. Both apartments at Mrs. Castle's had been occupied and the expedient thing for the Davieses to do had been to rent a house. In one of the new colonial developments they'd found a house with plenty of rooms and with a lawn which required more in the way of upkeep than had at first seemed likely. In the commotion of moving and then in the endless chores which this house seemed to provide for them to do, family matters were forgotten. Mrs. Castle saw much less of her family than she'd expected (their houses were almost on opposite sides of town) and Ian had frightening flashes where he saw himself, in his present situation, much more like the young couples (minus the marijuana) whom he'd had dinner with during his first assignment to the States than he'd ever expected to be. It had to do with the kind of house and the kind of neighborhood they were living in, he told himself, which acted almost like a drug and made all his speech and movement feel unnatural. He found himself asking young men from the office, especially Englishmen who were here on business, to the house for dinner, and he began to understand why he'd been asked so many times four years previously. Asking a couple over was asking for an elaborate performance, a brittle encounter in which conversation didn't flow but came in bursts—whereas a fellow on his own was more likely to fool around, to bring an air of relaxation and interest to the scene, which would strike him, just as it had struck Ian, as peculiar and intriguing. But, more than the changes which the new situation seemed to effect between him and Laura (the unreality of the social life made for a slight unreality in their treatment of each other), the biggest change between them had to do with Chris. This change, too, was connected with their being back in America.

In England Chris had seemed to Ian (and to Laura, too, presumably—she hadn't said otherwise) perfectly happy. He had made few friends and he apparently didn't miss them. Here in Waynesboro, so far, there were boys he knew, but after spending several afternoons with them, he'd lost interest and begun to go out of his way to avoid them whenever the opportunity offered. Laura's concern over this had come very suddenly out of nowhere (had she just not wanted to mention it in England?), and it also felt in some ways like a particularly American worry which Ian in part couldn't understand, but which was enough in the air so that he had begun worrying about it himself.

Laura came from a large family, with brothers and sisters and aunts and uncles scattered all over the States whom she never saw now, whom she hadn't in fact seen since she'd first married. But she still thought of them as having provided the mainstay of what security she'd had in her childhood, after her father had been killed. She worried at Chris's not having this sense of an extended family and she also worried about his being an only child. Ian, being an only child himself, failed to see what the problem was. He couldn't remember anyone ever worrying over his having no brothers and sisters or his having no friends—he knew he must have had friends of some sort, but he hadn't ever felt close to anyone until he got to university. He'd spent the greater part of his childhood on his own.

He knew that most children spent most of their time

with other children, but he also knew that there were children (he had been one of them and so was Chris, he felt—it was half the reason for his liking and taking an interest in Chris) who are quiet and spend most of their time on their own or among adults with whom they become, at an earlier age than is usual, equals. It seemed to him he had noticed this type of child in England more often than in the States (he couldn't think of any instance of it that he'd come across here so far, apart from Chris), but he had until now assumed that this was much more due to chance than to national character. But, with what seemed to him an unusual change in Laura and also with his growing inability to take any of the American men he came across seriously (the women were all right—some of them), he'd begun to think there was a great deal he didn't understand, a whole social instinct of which he was more ignorant than he, being after all married to an American, had previously been willing to admit. This sometimes made him feel that he was floundering and other times that he had his head screwed on right and that the people around him were all floundering, even if they didn't know it.

It happened again and again. He could think of examples. He could think of Bill Bray, for instance, who was a man Ian Davies liked as far as he could tell, which wasn't very far. Mr. Bray had, for someone who held a responsible and to some degree interesting job (for there must surely be *some* interest in being the manager of the branch of a bank), remarkably little to say, was shut up tight the whole time, might almost be thought of as perennially despondent, if it hadn't been for one or two eccentric, almost witty remarks he'd let drop to Mr. Davies at the occasional scout function which Ian and Laura had attended, remarks which, if he had been in

England, Ian Davies would have taken as social forays as well as hints of good conversation and good times to be had under different and more relaxed circumstances. Indeed he had taken them as forays and he and Laura had invited the Brays over for drinks, twice, and had never spent two such awkward evenings in their lives—no one saying a word, apart from Mrs. Bray complimenting Laura, every five minutes or so, on this or that bit of furniture or knickknack, of which there was not an abundance in the house, the compliments being delivered as though the best were being made of deplenished resources and adverse living conditions.

After several other similarly disastrous attempts at socializing with various different couples, Ian Davies was ready to give up. It seemed to him that the generally acknowledged stereotypes were way off the mark, were in fact almost the opposite of the actual state of things. In England, certainly, it might take a while to break through the ice, but once you were through you were through, whereas in America after you broke through the ice then you had to struggle through the glacier! No one talked! In his charitable moments he attributed this to the peculiar social sphere in which he traveled—a sphere of affluent technicians whose interest and inclination it was not to put into words what could be put into blueprints and formulas, an interest and inclination not representative of the country as a whole. But it seemed he could never get beyond this sphere and that this sphere might be all that there was, which led him, in his less charitable moments, to attribute the lack of intelligent talk not so much to the disinclination of a particular social sphere as to a general inability on a national scale, an attribution which the inane and illogical conversation of the few voluble individuals he came across (both the men and the women) only served to confirm.

There was Mr. Bray now, only thirty or forty feet away, and here was an opportunity to try again to play the friend. But really there was a certain kind of necessary energy and impulse lacking, missing altogether; any attempt at relaxation was bound to come across as contrived and somewhat forced, even condescending, and Ian Davies couldn't help thinking that the lack of energy was due only partially to discouragement on his own part; the rest was due to the very face that Mr. Bray put on, a face with which he didn't think anyone, English or American, would know how to cope—it was such a childish face. Mr. Davies gave it up, began to circulate aimlessly around the jamboree grounds, walking away from Mr. Bray. He found he simply didn't care. He made his move to avoid their possibly meeting.

The military band, too, had started to make a move and was marching, but in an orbit opposite to Mr. Davies's, progressing in circles toward an exact center of the jamboree ground, where Mr. Bray happened to be.

Mr. Bray caught wind of this progress and felt it, like a threat, coming toward him; he felt as though he were trying to walk along a log floating on a river and that he might slip off at any minute. The approach of the band seemed like the threat of a strong current against which all defenses would be null; it was bound to set the log spinning. He had an uneasy claustrophobic reaction to crowds, and on this occasion it was exaggerated by the heat which had been gathering this past hour and now had peaked, with the sun enclosing all the top of the sky, though at an angle, from the south: but with hardly a hint that the sun leaning south would mean winter soon. Sun was in people's arms as they bumped against him, and in their heads, and in the way they could see nothing with their eyes, which came to Mr. Bray with an overpowering tiredness and made the path he followed a blind one.

Sun was a visor that made sight as difficult as in a dream and made him think of Bill Jewitt. He had night-mares about Bill Jewitt, and these, along with the awful physical things that had stricken Bill, may have consti-tuted the dark side of the friendship, the side that, in his conscious reminiscence, Mr. Bray did not explore. He had dreams that Bill Jewitt (looking as powerful and effective as he had in high school) persuaded him to exchange his own sound pair of legs for the shattered ones. All the implications of having shattered legs froze Mr. Bray in his dream and woke him with a start; every time he woke he lay paralyzed in bed till he could gather enough nerve to try to move. He had a dream in which, under the guise of its being some adventure like they'd had in the old days, Bill Jewitt led him to the wickerwork basket of a helium balloon, helped him in, and then cut the rope connecting the basket to earth, sending Mr. Bray floating much higher than he had ever intended to go, while Bill Jewitt stood on the ground in a cornfield, naked, getting smaller and smaller, and watching, as though to mark under what circumstance the contents of the basket might finally spill. This was, in an odd way, an erotic dream, but it brought only a feeling of vertigo without any hint of pleasure.

Mr. Bray never mentioned these dreams to anyone — for the very good reason that he had no one to mention them to. It didn't even occur to him that such things were speakable or could be given a certain portion of his own or someone else's attention and credited with an existence if not an actual meaning. His dreams took place in a vacuum. No matter how violent their movement, they had no acknowledgeable face or shape. The dreams were building, were building, it was not just the night that brought them now, but odd disturbing things in the daytime that seemed to be setting them free and letting them get closer, as if these images previously had been chained, safely and obdurately, far, far away. The sun, unconscious, radiating from young boys' arms; the quivering, knobbly, lashed poles used as the basic support of a rope bridge scouts were attempting to cross at this jamboree; the sight, two weeks ago, in the dank tunnel corridor that led from the PATH subway platform to Pennsylvania Station, of a sorry old derelict in a raincoat, with newspapers cluttered around him, his head sunk to one side, unshaven, his shoulders propped up against a tile wall, and the rest of his body slouched, legs extending out flat into the pedestrian thoroughfare—all these things brought Mr. Bray's dreams of Bill Jewitt to the surface, vividly, as if he could see them right before his eyes or taste them dry and portentous on his tongue, and created yet another obstacle, like his weekly encounters with Mr. Cantwell, for him to overcome.

Now he saw a knot-tying contest, a relay race of sorts, with boys sprinting up and down and tying knots on blue stakes pounded into the ground. Older scouts, some of them Explorers, stood by as judges or, rather, inspectors, ensuring that the knots had been tied correctly. The crowds surrounding this event cheered and urged the members of their own troops on, and yet these shouts of encouragement were beside the point. When a boy got to the stake and knelt down to try to get his knot done, you could see what mattered, you could see him abstract himself, find himself alone with the ends of rope in his fingers, ends of finger and rope sometimes getting confused so that, like Daedalus, he might almost be spinning himself out of himself, the air all round giving so many clues. It was some part of him, not his head by any means, but more like the power of grip in his arms, telling him which clues to select and in which order they would become the right ones. The knots got progressively more difficult as the contest went on.

Meanwhile, Mr. Wing (unlike Mr. Bray, who'd forgotten about the very existence of his sons, let alone their present whereabouts and activity) was spying on his oldest son, Mark, who was representing Troop 431 in a fire-building contest.

Fire building was, within the troop, Mark's one real forte. On winter camping trips when everything was iced over or buried in snow, on rain-soaked spring or fall trips when you got so wet that trickles of water ran from inside the hood of your poncho down the nape of your neck and small of your back and down the bridge of your nose to your nose's tip, where it dripped, dripped, dripped, Mark could always be counted on to conjure up a fire in ten minutes flat—as long as the matches weren't wet. And Mark usually had better luck than anyone else in the troop in keeping matches dry. Matches were something he could handle, he had them on his person at all times, flames were something he could arrange, fire might almost be a secret power he drew on, something he carried hidden in the palm of his hand, in his timidity in facing the outside world. Only once had he abused this power and on that occasion he'd gotten a reprimand so emphatic, so severe, that from then on he'd carried himself more covertly than ever.

In Waynesboro there had been, for some time, a practice of making all elementary, grammar, junior-high, and high schools the targets of phantom nuclear attacks at least once every two months. Phantom nuclear attacks being more impressive phenomena than mere fire drills, a siren was installed especially for the purpose at Mark's school to warn of their approach, instead of relying on the usual fire bell. Also, and perhaps this too was due to differences in the characters of the two emergencies as perceived by the school's principal (a man who always had reasons for every bureaucratic move he made, which, however unfounded in reality, were strangely persuasive and ardently held), phantom nuclear attacks always came at two-thirty in the afternoon on Friday, just before school let out, whereas fire drills almost always occurred on Tuesdays at ten in the morning.

There were two different procedures for dealing with nuclear raids, although there was no real logic as to which of them was used when. Sometimes these raids meant that students had to slip under their desks and hide their heads between their knees, with their hands folded protectively over the backs of their necks. Under the desks, everyone stayed very quiet and still—one was given the impression that the greatest thing to worry about was getting glass in the back of your neck. It was better to get glass in your hands than in your neck. The people in the row of desks next to the huge glass windows stayed particularly still and clasped their necks very tightly.

The second and more rarely used of the two procedures was for the teachers and students and clerical staff to make a collective withdrawal to the Tunnel. There ran beneath the school a tunnel (whether built specifically for the purpose of escaping phantom nuclear air raids or to hide from some other threatening disaster cannot be said) whose long, dark, claustrophobic course came in welcome contrast, especially in summer, to the brightly lit and stern open air of the classrooms. There were things that thinking about the tunnel could teach you that you'd never learn in a million years listening to a teacher's voice or even looking out a classroom window. On the days when the siren sounded and it was the tunnel in which they were to take refuge rather than under their desks, everyone congregated in the auditorium (dark and gloomy during the day, unlit for these occasions) and in the corridors outside the auditorium, and then, after everything had been organized and all persons accounted for, everyone slipped two by two, three by three, through an entrance which was just to the right of the stage apron, until the entire student population and staff were underground. They would stay down there for as long as twenty minutes or half an hour, and then the all-clear would sound and they'd come back up into light, first of the schoolrooms' fluorescent sheen and then of the sun outside, where the buses would be waiting to take them home.

On one of these drills, Mark's had been the first class to enter the tunnel, and Mark had been in the very front of the line. He had wandered far ahead, much farther than he'd ever been on previous drills, to where folding chairs stored neatly along the side of the corridor gave way to scraps of wood, bits and pieces from long ago, things which made you think of classrooms your parents or grandparents might have been in, because this school was as old as that. It had been built in the Depression, and it looked it, too: enormous, dull, made of brick. He'd passed beneath the oily smell and thunder of the furnace room, on and on, until he'd come to the end of the tunnel, the last fifty yards of which had been totally dark—there were no more lights. At the end of the tunnel was a sudden and greater accumulation of broken chairs and scrap wood than there had been all along the way, and there were chips and sawdust too. He'd taken out his penlight and, by its thin ray, examined the debris, considered the dark—and then set to work.

While he worked, he thought of the air-raid drills where you didn't come down to the tunnel but stayed upstairs; he thought bitterly of the injustice of his teacher, a woman of twenty-five, having a bigger and better desk to hide beneath (for the teachers rarely lost time in practicing hiding, once they'd seen all their students crouching down), until he remembered and derived a secret comfort from a bit of information he'd picked up from one of his father's scientific journals. This was that nuclear rays would find you no matter where you were; they would come through windows, through brick, through paint, through wood, it didn't matter if you tried to hide from them, and if you didn't die from them just now, you'd die from them twenty years later. Knowing and remembering this made it easier to work at trying to get rid of the darkness. He could see, in his mind, just the kind of light he was going to make. The walls would absorb it and be yellow, and his shadow would be cast upon the walls and move and stretch in proportion to the flames moving and stretching; his shadow would be a thing that would wrap around the light, which was a thing that would make walls seem liquid.

But he got no further than building a criss-cross of chips and kindling and striking the first match before his teacher (who had accounted for all her little troop but one and who didn't *like* being this far inside the tunnel, farther than anyone else) caught sight of the flame, panicked (who knew what kind of dreadful inflammable fumes there might be down here, accumulated from all these years), and rushed toward Mark, yelling, "Goddamnit no!" but not at all in the same way as Mr. Gough might have yelled it (the way Mr. Gough yelled it could be almost comforting, reassuring at times; it let you know that Mr. Gough was still Mr. Gough). She yelled it in a way which was most unlike her and which scared Mark badly, especially since he was a quiet, well-behaved boy who hadn't ever had even the slightest reprimand from her before.

Nowadays, before he lit a fire, he always looked around at the people and the air in the vicinity, as if to make sure there was no darkness there to dispel, this being what he thought had been his crime.

The contest finished quickly. Mark got his fire started (Mr. Wing, although he'd sworn he'd stay at the far back of the crowd, had pushed right to the front, his blue eyes intent, his mustache wavering, his thinning bright orange hair all wild and astray; he'd even shouted, "Go!") more quickly than anyone else, bringing in the only first prize that a Troop 431 member was to win that weekend. But, after he got his ribbon, he didn't stick around to celebrate his victory. Instead he slunk off, found his two younger brothers, proposed something to them, and they all went off together. There was a nature trail that went through the holly forest and then, on a boardwalk, through a swampy area, and he wanted to explore it before it was crowded with other scouts. His younger brothers always followed Mark in anything he did, confident that, for the most part, Mark was even more grownup and sensible than their father — who could still be silly, especially with their mother, on occasion. At least, this was the way they, having never strayed beyond Mark's influence, saw his mysterious power to command them.

His sons' disappearance left Mr. Wing aimlessly

wandering around the center of the jamboree grounds, over which, now, a gull swung slowly up.

Mr. Berringer's hole was as deep as it could be; it was a thing he had entered into. He had the Dutch oven, charred and crusted over with sootblack of past fires, at his side. Periodically he inserted it, considered it in the hole, then altered the course of his digging a little, trying to achieve the perfect fit, the perfect dimension.

Mr. Gough, for his part, had found himself powerfully drawn to the archery competition.

The gull soared, hovered, looped, swayed back down. Everything seemed to wait. White wings made an utter ease of the air . . . and then were flayed, torn apart, figuratively at least, by sound.

Sound came. Awful sound.

Low, very low over the Hook, much lower than anything yet (and metallic, screaming) a formation of six diminutive fighter jets had flown past, curved black and steely claws ripping across the sky, lithe, swift, like the cleverest flick of the wrist, uncombing things, then quickly turning on their sides and coming back over, engines making a sound of razors, to greet these boys on their day of festivities and so, incidentally, to do a bit of advertising.

All the boys on that site looked up, even Jim Gough, whose hand went out to catch for balance where there was nothing to catch. Then, when what he was reaching for turned out to be air, his whole body began to lose its hold: he was walking over a rope bridge, where the contest was to get across without using your hands. With a violent wrench he was able to get himself straight but not without touching, just grazing, for a moment the hand rope with his elbow and his wrist. All this felt slow, not half so fast as it was, so that really it was surprising that so many boys (of those who were judging the contest) caught sight of the transgression, what with the disturbance of the fighter jets above, and had the presence of mind to accuse in unison, "Disqualified!" as they had done with every other contestant in this event, it being an impossible task they had set to be done.

The fighter jets vanished as suddenly as they had appeared, leaving a low rumble in the sky.

The gull still drifted down.

The archery event was, to Mr. Gough's mind, the most interesting event of those going on here. Archery was a skill he appreciated more than fire building or knot tying. But he wished these boys had something better than a mere stuffed target to aim at, something in motion perhaps, something in flight.

Boys, scattering from events and games which were petering out now, were drawn irresistibly to the bunkers, with their steep sides and fabulous views at the top, where they played war, devised and then acted upon "strategies," stalked and snooped for phantom Krauts, Japs, and Commies.

The gull gave a mew.

And the word "disqualified" hung in air which, having been filled with noise, now felt padded over, as though someone had put cotton in everyone's ears.

The judges, on the chance that no one had heard them the first time (for Jim Gough was still carrying on as if he might win), repeated loudly, for all to hear, "*Disqualified!*"

Jim gave a long look to the side, ten feet above where anyone could be, as if to see who was accusing him, and still carried on, reaching the end of the bridge now as if he had done the feat in perfect accordance with the rules throughout.

But the younger boys wouldn't let him go without his acknowledging them. They were enamored of just deserts and of the sound of the word too, and they sang it faster and faster, with great and greater emphasis as they went:

Dis-*qua*lified! Dis-*qua*lified!

Jim looked at them with a sneer; he swaggered, almost as if they were saying he had won and he was having to show them he didn't care. Their voices piped higher, repeating and repeating, until the whole crowd was shouting with a strange accent and rhythm beyond the meaning of the word, a powerful military emotion filling their voices with its sound; and the sound went:

*Squa*lified! di-
*Squa*lified! di-
*Squa*lified! di-
*Squa*lified!

The sound went on and on. Jim's sneer turned to real rage. He leaped down from the end of the rope bridge, hurled to the ground a small scout who happened to be standing there vacantly chanting the word, and then stalked off, shaking several people from him (even an Explorer scout who tried to collar him, perhaps for further punishment) as he went. At the edge of the crowd that had gathered around the rope bridge, one last person grabbed hold of him as if to give him something of what he had coming, and Jim whipped around, put a menacing fist in his face, grabbed and wrenched his shirt collar up tight too. Then he just as violently let go, turned around, and strode away, like an angry horse or engine, panting, till he was a diminutive figure, things (tents, trucks, flagpoles) beginning to cross the path between the crowd's position and his, until, finally, he was farther off than it was worth their while to think about or go. Whereupon, like a shadow that had passed through their midst and, with its passing, left everyone relieved, or like a week of harsh, inclement weather, not only compensated for but totally obliterated by a day of sun and brilliance, they promptly forgot about him.

The flag (but what kind of flag was it?) continued to flutter aimlessly from its pole, high up, displaying a wavering, uncertain outline, sharp against the sky, against the blue.

Boys scrambled up and down these bunkers, then, called them dunes, and used them for fields of imaginary battle. They died and came back to life again, died and then fought on an opposite side in a different war. Some boys, the youngest ones, stood at the bottom of the bunkers, near dark entrances, as though lost, uncertain of where to shoot, who to kill, and liable, in one or two of the most pathetic cases, to cry if someone, after uttering a machine-gun staccato—"*Eh-eh-eh-eh-eh-eh-eh-eh-eh-eh!*"—were to emerge from thick bushes and address them: "Lie down—I got you—you been killed."

However, not all the boys were able to stay immersed in their war games—at least, not all the boys who were able to achieve the summit of the "dune," for from up there the voices of the jamboree were distant, the air moved with a different candor, there was strong inducement to fall quiet, to look and contemplate the view all around you, it came about naturally.

It was up here, and quietly at first, that the unlikely trio of Billy and Roger Bray and Chris Castle found

themselves gathered. Chris had not been involved with
the war games but had made his way up here in spite of
them, shrugging his shoulders and smiling when boys
younger than he was emerged from hiding to inform him
that he was dead. It reminded him of a boy at school
whose house he had visited once (and been too bored
the one time ever to go back and visit again) who
owned literally hundreds of small plastic soldiers and
toy tanks and every other kind of military paraphernalia
imaginable, with which he'd conducted campaigns for
an entire afternoon, as he apparently did every afternoon
of the week, for he offered Chris no word of introduction
to this activity: almost as if he assumed this was what
everyone did each day when he got home from school.
Great sieges and routs led from the garage to the living
room, from the den to the bedrooms, in and out of the
kitchen and all the bathrooms (there were three and a
half of these, as Americans put it), and at the end (after
a kind of blitz which involved his pouncing on the
amassed innumerable plastic bodies and rolling around
on them as if to smear them into the rug) he announced
in firm authoritative tones, "You can go home now—the
Nazis won this time," as though that were his secret
wish, his private fantasy.

Chris had gotten to the top of the bunker first and
was discovered there by the Bray twins only minutes
later. The Bray twins may have entered a little, on their
way up the bunker, into the war games, but if they did it
was most likely in a spirit of genial and, at their best,
hilarious parody. Rough as they could be (which really
wasn't all that rough but fierce and fast; it was their
pace more than anything else which distinguished them),
anything which smacked of organization (and there was
always someone who'd take it on himself to start giving

orders in these affairs) was always distasteful to them. If violence appealed to them at all, it was really a fluid, sensual kind of violence, as in wrestling or, as their adventure with Mindy Gough had revealed to them only weeks ago, as in sex of all different kinds, not in the dry organized violence and tactics of imaginary guns. The violence which appealed to them was the kind which, in its natural rhythm, alternated with the profoundest peace: a sudden subsidence and looking around, which had no less satiating an effect than a wild leap or cry or outburst of activity.

This sudden subsidence was what they entered now, for some unknown reason, upon seeing Chris, as if Chris were the catalyst. The three of them stood and slowly turned around, always looking out. On the side of the bunkers away from the jamboree was a margin of salt marsh (with cattails growing high, with rusting oil drums and rotten car tires caught in their midst, abandoned by some tide), and beyond that was Raritan Bay and the low New Jersey shoreline. Looking in the opposite direction, beyond the holly forest, a fringe of natural sand dunes could be seen (not very high compared to up here) and, beyond that, the blue ocean with ships on it. To the north, they could see the shape of the Hook getting wider and then petering out, with low green-painted barracks of a military camp at its tip, and beyond that, where the air began to haze, five or ten miles off, the big bridge spanning the Narrows between Brooklyn and Staten Island. Very far away, so far that you could hardly see them at all, the twin towers of the World Trade Center loomed high like two building blocks stood on end by a child with no sense of proportion, no feel for design at all. The towers were out of keeping with the earth, out of keeping with the air, but still were interesting to see, seeming as they did superimposed on the skyline, scale models introduced into a set of models of a smaller scale.

"That's New York," Chris informed them. "That's the Verrazano-Narrows Bridge—but I don't think we can see the Empire State Building."

The Bray twins took this in; they looked, impressed with the sight of a city they had heard so much about but had only been to on rare occasions and under painfully close supervision. It was a place they wanted to go to, a place they were working toward, but even so it caught only a certain part of their imagination and, being boys still, it wasn't long before they, irresistibly, turned to look at the ocean.

Chris caught this change of their direction and thought to explain that too.

"Europe's that way," he said and pointed just a little to the left of where they were looking.

They all looked out in silence. Europe was at the other side of what they were seeing, at the other side of the ocean, and they all knew what Europe was. But the solemnity with which they looked became too great, it was oppressive, looking at things was something that there was no reason to do for too long, and it got Roger Bray started jumping up and down, dancing, and chanting, "I see Europe! I see France! I see the Eiffel Tower!"

Chris turned to him, said in all seriousness, "You can't, it's too far—" but then looked in that same direction, to see what it was he *might* be seeing. There was nothing. A few boats moved like slow chess pieces across the horizon.

Billy Bray came back at him (while Roger still danced,

shouted, "I see the Alps! I see Italy! I see Africa! I see Idi Amin!") and took him up: "How d'you know? You're not American."

"Yes I am."

"What did the elephant say to the other elephant who was standing in the shower?"

"I don't know—what?"

"'No soap—radio.'"

Chris laughed.

Billy said, "You laughed. You're not supposed to laugh. It's a joke where you're not supposed to laugh. You can't be American."

"Well, I am."

"How can you be?"

"My mom's American and my dad was American."

Here, Billy Bray thought, was where Chris Castle had surely tripped up over the obvious fact, evident to all. "No he's not."

"That's not my dad. That's my stepdad. My real dad was American."

"Where is he then?"

"He's dead."

Quick, and this brought everything quiet.

"Anyway," Chris continued after a moment, "you can't even see *Bermuda* from here and that's closest of all," which won the twins' confidence since their parents had honeymooned in Bermuda (it was a high point in the family photograph album) and they both knew that their mother could never have persuaded their father to go too far, so that Billy asked Chris, "Why's he dead?"

"He got killed—in a war."

Billy, to this answer, could almost have done his bazooka imitation and made a joke of everything that existed in the world, but there was something in the look of curiosity with which Roger, calmed down now, was addressing Chris that made him desist and after a moment instead ask, "Which war?"

To which Chris replied, "In Vietnam."

There was a kind of conference between the twins, and it was Roger who was able to supply the missing information.

"*Commies . . .* " he whispered.

Which Billy Bray took up in no uncertain terms. "How come you don't sound American then?"

"It's my accent," Chris explained, and seemed almost to point to where this might be, in the side of his neck.

"Where'd you live before you lived here?"

"In England—but we took lots of holidays." And then having triumphantly gotten through all the questions put to him, he put a question to them in turn; he asked, "Do you know what *this* is?" and pointed straight down to the earth on which they were standing.

"It's the ground."

"No, I mean—"

"It's a sand dune."

"No it's not, it's a—"

"Okay, what is it?"

"It's a bunker."

"I knew that."

"Then why didn't you say?"

"And it was used to kill Commies."

"I don't think it was ever used," Chris said and looked around, as if for evidence. "It doesn't *look* like it's been used."

"How would you know?"

"We took holidays everywhere. We took a bicycle

holiday in Holland. There's bunkers in all the dunes, wired off, most of them, but some of them you can get in. Only you've got to watch out for mines."

"Mines?"

"You step on one and *wham!*" he made a gesture with his hands, "it'll blow you up."

"See? It killed Commies."

"Not *this* one—the ones I'm talking about." There was a feeling of growing belligerence between them which Chris was tempted and succumbed into aggravating by adding, "And besides it was Nazis not Commies over there."

"Nazis—Commies—same difference. Shoot 'em with a bazooka," Billy replied and—"blowie! blowie! blowie! blowie!"—wheeled in a circle firing off the imaginary bazooka from waist level into the dormant air.

There was no reply to this, so Chris put another question to them, addressed them both:

"What did you do with Mindy Gough in the tunnel?"

For that was where this adventure, too, was supposed to have taken place, in almost the same spot as Mark Wing's. He addressed them both, because it was supposed to have been both of them who had gone down there with her, but at first it was only Roger, as though he were the one with expertise in these matters, who replied.

He smirked virtuously and said, "It wasn't in the tunnel, it was in the cellar at our house. What we did was—"

"We all held hands—Jim, too," Billy interrupted.

Two identical faces, bright and ingenuous, waited and stared to gauge Chris's reaction. And Chris's eyes widened because he hadn't known Jim was in on it too; until finally they couldn't hold it back anymore, they fell apart with laughing, they were helpless, the laughter fell into the air and was giggles and snorts, made them roll around, until sun was the echo of it and had them hopeless, spinning, used up until they were exhausted. Chris smiled in the most genial way possible and even started to laugh at the violence of some of their paroxysms, but he quieted down well before they did and sat down to wait for them, as if for further information.

But any further information was not forthcoming.

The twins had just about regained their breath and were muttering half words to each other: "Didja? didja? —waddya, waddya ... " when Roger suddenly gave a gasp of real terror.

In an instant Billy was on him to pound whatever it was away, to death, but Chris saw it too, slipped nimbly in between, and plucked it out.

Roger, still panicking, said, "Jesus!" and Billy, sitting up now, added, "Christ!"

"It's only a glass snake," Chris said. "See?" He held the snake out to them. "My granddad told me to watch out for them over here. He showed me in a book. It looks like a snake but it's actually a lizard—a legless lizard."

This information was hard to believe. Chris seemed a veritable mine of questionable facts. Both Brays looked at him holding and handling the lizard–snake, they watched him let it twine around his fingers, and then they looked at Chris's eyes, where there was something so clear and focused and steady, so calming that a complete quiet was regained among the three of them once more.

Down below, in the campsite, whistles were blown, and voices were calling, and even bugles were being played, but none of it seemed to reach up here—or only in the most ineffectual way.

"Here, you want to hold it?"

Billy took the creature from Chris's fingers.

"Careful now, don't squash it."

The snake tried to escape Billy's grasp.

"Let it go where it wants to go. I'll catch it if you lose it."

Billy let it slide through a constant movement and reversal of hands, under, over, until finally it wove entirely off, fell to the ground.

Chris snapped it back up, however.

"Roger?"

Roger didn't want to hold the glass snake.

Chris went on with his demonstration: "What do you bet if I hold it by its tail its tail falls off?"

Neither of them answered this, but only watched.

"Look . . ."

Chris held the creature over the ground by its tail. And a moment later it was gone and Chris was showing them something in his palm.

"I'll have to write my granddad, tell him where we found it."

"Where's your granddad live?" This was an accusation. Who would have a grandfather living more than ten miles away from them? Both of the Brays' grandfathers were only five minutes away by car.

"In England."

"He's English then!"

Immediately the inquisition was on again, but friendlier this time, more like a game; this was a point scored.

And Chris enjoyed answering, "He's not my real granddad, he's Ian's dad."

"Who's Ian?"

"Ian's my stepdad."

"Mr. Davies?"

"Yes."

"His name's Ian?"

"Yes."

"How d'you spell it?"

"I.A.N.—Ian." Chris sat as if to dare any other question they might have.

"Where's your real granddad?"

"He's dead."

"He's dead too?"

"We went to see where he got killed."

"Where'd he get killed?"

Chris repeated the question "Where'd he get killed?," only not so much as a demand for information, but as a statement of doubt, as if the whereabouts were uncertain. He tried, for a moment, to remember the place's name. But, at this, the thought and then the image of a gray day, a world away, rose up before him, the image of a flat gray sky with green-gray land beneath; it was a low plateau at the edge of the sea. At its top there was a formal garden with white gravel paths and green lawns kept trimmed and smooth as felt. There were marble tombstones, too, white and smooth, placed at two-foot intervals along the lawns. He remembered walking among big marble monuments and then past row upon row of the small stone markers, some of them with names on them, others blank. He had been with his mother and Ian, but he had walked ahead of them slightly, while they looked for something. The rows of stone markers came to an end and then there were some steps which led down bluffs toward a beach, but the steps never reached the beach; this was a dream landscape. The steps simply reached a lookout point, a balcony from which one could see the landscape reverting from this imposed formality to its more natural state. And what the balcony looked out upon, beyond the beach, in the gray water, very still, making a soft susurrant sound in the surf, were the hulks of half-sunken ships that had been left where they were as a reminder of war. They were like the pieces of a half-finished puzzle that would neither be completed nor submit to the process of scattering. A hand seemed poised in the sky, hidden just above the overcast's flat gray surface, unable to rearrange them, and this made the hulks terribly disturbing, set as they were. Chris saw them and remembered the same hulks in a war film, a documentary, that he'd watched on the BBC. The gray on the screen seemed to have had nothing to do with its being a black-and-white set he had watched this program on, but with the grayness of the place itself, which he imagined was always gray—and far removed from anything else. On the screen there'd been the hulks, but with men on them and leaving them in landing boats and sounds of gunfire on this bluff and beach where Chris stood in eerie quiet now. Faces had passed chaotically in and out of camera shot and there had appeared for a split second a face as to whose identity, brief as the appearance was, Chris had no doubt. It was a young man's face, the face of a man just turned thirty, his grandfather's, whose picture he had seen at his grandmother's house in Maryland, looking groomed and smart, frozen, in his uniform. Chris had thought that that was what was meant by being dead—being frozen. But the face on the screen had been moving almost faster than you could see, in and out of camera range, and also changing expression, veering between terror and intention, veering around. He'd run to his mother and told her what he'd seen and she'd said it couldn't possibly be true. When he insisted that he *had* seen him, seen his grandfather, his mother had said that even if that were true there would never be any way to find out and know for sure, which made the face and the hulks like things which you fell back through every time you thought of them. And falling back through them made Chris think in turn of the place where his father had been killed, a place he'd never seen and probably never would see, a place in another climate altogether, a place in which, when he imagined it, Chris felt he might get lost—was already in, already lost, just at the thought of it. Your eye wandered round and circled in and then got fixed, sank into this one bleak spot.

But the Brays pulled him out of it. They asked again, of his grandfather, eager to know, "Yeah, where'd he get killed?"

And Chris answered them this time: "In France, in Normandy."

They thought about this, and then Roger softly made the comment "Boy, a lot of people in your family sure are dead."

Billy asked, "Is your mother dead?"

"No, she's still alive" was the cheerful answer. And he added, "She married my stepdad," as though this were further proof.

"You call your stepdad Ian?" Roger asked, backtracking a little.

"Yes." And then to embarrass them, showing off the advantage of dealing with your guardian on a first-name basis, he asked them, knowing perfectly well what the answer would be, having seen them with their father on every camping trip these last nine months, "Why? What do you call your dad?" as though there were a possibility of their calling him something even more unusual than his name, which was Billy's name, "William."

But "We call our dad Dad" was what they answered, oblivious of the fact that Chris must surely have noticed this before. They were rapt with him now, rapt with the game. With every move in it, it seemed, there was a deflection: Death. And with every deflection there was a substitute: a "stepdad" or a "step-granddad." They couldn't imagine what came next, what strategy, what direction. They could only wait for him to explain it a little more. And, shortly, he began again to do so.

"I'm the only one left with my dad's name, Castle. Not even my mother has it now. She's got Ian's name. She's had three names—hers, my Dad's, and Ian's."

He let them take this in for a moment, and then he added, somewhat irrelevantly but impressively, "A man's home is his castle," a proverb he'd always thought of as applying especially to him.

Since they had nothing to say to this either, he went on, omnisciently, "You can get *inside* bunkers, you know."

"You can't get inside this one," Billy answered.

"Why not?"

"Can you?"

"I bet there're people inside it already."

"But what about mines?" Roger asked.

Mines had evidently made an impression.

"The Germans never got this far," Chris replied, as though this made for an obvious absence of mines; and then, eying them both, he challenged them.

"Come on!"

He got up, took a few paces, then looked back to see if they were following him. He hadn't ever done this, he hadn't ever taken charge like this before. He had always been in someone or something else's charge. They looked at him.

"Come on," he said, low and urgent this time.

They got to their feet, came to him.

"Come on where?"

"We can go inside."

"Is it dark inside?"

"Of course it's dark."

"We'll need a flashlight."

"Roger can go get one."

They all three clambered down until they were again on a level with the jamboree, and then they sent Roger sprinting back to the Troop 431 campsite to find a flashlight. Roger met Mr. Berringer there, still working on his arrangement for the Dutch oven, with piles of sandy earth at his side now and almost all the troop's cooking equipment spread around him. He looked up from his project when Roger came tearing in, dived into a tent, found a flashlight in no time, and then popped out, about to take off.

Mr. Berringer asked, "Where're you going?" not so much in his supervisory capacity as out of simple curiosity.

And Roger had just the answer that neither satisfied nor cried out for deterrence. "Going exploring!" he said.

Mr. Berringer's lifted gaze followed Roger almost like a benison, as if any exploration on which the boy embarked could only be a good and noble thing.

Roger met his twin and Chris Castle at the entrance of the bunker, panting but triumphant, holding the light.

The first thing Billy said was "It's been on."

Chris and Roger looked, and saw that indeed it had been on. Roger turned the light off and then back on to see what the contrast was. It wasn't much. Still, "It'll be brighter in the dark—always is," he predicted, an optimist.

"Did you turn it on while you were carrying it or was it on in the tent?" his brother asked him.

He answered twice: "Dunno. I dunno."

The question dampened his spirits a little.

Billy saw this, took pity on him, confiscated the light, examined it more closely, and finally pronounced, "It'll do," in the way that their mother might have pronounced the final favorable verdict on a piece of kitchen gadgetry given as a gift on Mother's Day, if the verdict wasn't actually "We'll have to take it back."

And, because this qualified statement was really a seal of one hundred percent approval as far as actual results were concerned, Roger perked up, began to bounce, shift from one foot to another.

"Let's go."

Chris led the way.

They had to scrape through a bit of barbed wire, but it wasn't hard. The wire was old and had come loose from the fence it was tied into. Chris held it open for the twins and then for himself to slip through without touching. There was almost a little paddock, grassy, overgrown, wired in, in front of the bunker entrance. They waded through the high grass.

Then they were in the bunker—daylight behind them and darkness ahead.

"Let me get to the front," Chris said. "Roger get in back and shine the light on the ground so we can see."

The three of them in line, in this designated order, began to move then, to probe. They went twenty yards or so, then turned a corner to the left. All sound was removed and what was left was an abyss, an empty echo, much closer to whoever or whatever had been in here ages before than to whatever was going on right now outside. They could hear their own steps and their own breathing, and then they turned another corner, to the right this time. A dim shaft of light came down a number of yards ahead, and when they got to it they looked up and saw brilliant blue sky, incredibly brilliant blue, a precisely demarked square foot of it, with weeds hanging over.

"They shouldn't leave a shaft open like that," Chris said. "We were up there."

With the light, sound came in, but it was only the sound of wind, and it made the Present seem farther away than ever.

They walked on.

Roger made a nervous sound, giggled, and then said, "Spooks."

Billy made sounds of ghosts, creaking doors, death rattles, until he suddenly went quiet—realizing there was no one but themselves to scare.

Chris said nothing, but both Billy and Roger could somehow sense he approved of the lapse back into quiet.

It got darker, the shaft of light was far behind; they turned another corner.

The bunker seemed much bigger inside than had ever looked possible from the outside.

The flashlight began to fail, was only a ghost of a light.

"Put your hand on my shoulder; I can see," Chris instructed Billy. "Roger, put your hand on Billy's shoulder." But how he could see, what he was following, there was no way of telling, it was a secret to himself. The lack of light was coming close to matching the absence of all sounds, the absence of all but their own sounds, and those were slow, hesitant in the extreme, except for the silent and patient steps of Chris, whose progress (Billy could tell by the feel of his shoulder) seemed confident, assured, undaunted—through the lack of light. . . .

Where Jim Gough walked, when he walked away from the rope bridge, was right out of the campsite, right away from the jamboree, into the holly forest, following a path which led through there. His head skimmed a ceiling of leaves, thick and endless, like a vast spreading arbor, so that he had to keep stooped. A hummingbird hovered in his path for a moment (he'd never seen one of those before) and then took off. The holly woods had the feel of something firm balanced over shifting ground, something much more permanent and primeval than seemed in keeping with a sand spit, something difficult to twist or break. At their very center Jim took off his cap, his neckerchief, and his shirt, and hung them on a branch. This left him in only his T-shirt and scout pants, which had faded from their original khaki-green, so that he could go out unmarked into the world. He got to the other edge of the woods quickly and soon was walking down the Hook's main road, almost bouncing as he went.

What he bounced on was the sun suffused in the air and its being three o'clock on an afternoon rising with an energy which he didn't know how to disperse, but he would try.

Things bothered him here that hadn't bothered him back in the campsite, such as sweat running down his back, or flies, some of them horseflies, gathering in a cloud around his head (he supposed all the flies in the campsite had made straight for the latrines as soon as these had been set up and put to use). But, whereas in the campsite these discomforts would only have made him irritable and made him want to pick on McDaniels or on Chris Castle (who was beginning distinctly to annoy him by being always so right and yet not good for anything), here they made him want to lunge and tumble, grip and throw, wrestle, and that was for the strength of it, that was to be strong. Sun was to be swung at, and three o'clock (or maybe just a little before or after three —he had no watch) was time enough for all the world.

When at last he got off the dirt road which led up the Hook and was walking along the shoulder of the highway, with cars speeding all their different colors past, he sighed a little, breathed the deep fumes, relieved at being back in the arms of civilization. The highway followed the sandy edge of the sea, ran along an island beach with the ocean on one side and a sound on the other, dividing it from the mainland. Billboards were spaced at intervals along the sound side; they advertised motel accommodations, fishing equipment and ocean bait, an amusement park with a water slide, and a miniature golf course open twenty-four hours a day. There were beach houses that *looked* like beach houses, trashier and flimsier and more crowded together than the houses overlooking Raritan Bay that they'd passed in their cars that morning.

Here too, half a mile or so farther on, were the advertised motels, with door numbers rusted and come loose from their nails on marine-blue painted doors, and with signs in crowded parking lots which said NO VACANCIES in plastic lettering that was meant to be illuminated by neon which no longer worked—and just fifty yards ahead there was a liquor store squeezed between two of the motels. It was in here that Jim Gough went.

He bought a bottle of red wine.

A boy his own age didn't bother him over the question of I.D., but gave him a look, which Jim returned, as he picked the bottle up off the counter and left.

He waited for a pause in the traffic, then crossed the road. Between the ocean and the road there was a strip of piled sand, with very little in the way of dune grass growing on it, sand dunes which looked as though they'd been washed away by rain or worn away by footsteps and constricted by their proximity to the road on one side and the construction of a boardwalk on the other. Jim Gough didn't care. He walked through the sand, crossed the boardwalk, and got to the level beach, then walked down through crowds of sun and ocean bathers, families and couples on their usual summer's-end last grab at freedom before work and study and long dreary winter set in. Ocean and land came up against each other in a mood of festivities. Land seemed almost to be shooting streamers out into the air over the water and, as if to confirm this, a small plane came from over the low brow of the first inland hill and headed out to sea. No one on the crowded beach noticed it, however, except for Jim, whose eyes followed it and took it as a secret confirmation, a slow path in the air.

It occurred to him, after a while, that he stood out here almost as much as he would have if he'd kept in full uniform. Everyone was in a brightly colored bathing suit. Mothers and fathers eyed Jim in his T-shirt and trousers, apprehensive as to what trouble he might make, and it was this, on other occasions, that had made Jim angry, angry that it was always assumed he brought trouble with him wherever he was, whereas it seemed obvious to him, looking at it clearly and objectively, that trouble came to him, pulled him up and found him out; it could make him burn with anger, anger at their not seeing he had no hand in it. But not just now, not on this day, not under this sky. He even smiled at kids digging deep, covered in liquid sand, who offered him a plastic shovel as he went by as they would instantly have offered it to any stranger going past, until they were taught how not to.

Looking at the way they offered him all they had, everything that was in their hands, he had to concede that, when trouble came to him, he wouldn't turn his back on it or run away or slip past it, but would take it on as he would have taken on someone who had exasperated him and, this time, would have to be taught a lesson. Unfortunately, although he was only fifteen (an age at which victory of a sort or at least the illusion of imminent victory, more than at any other age, can be expected), he had, up until now, had a consistent losing streak, he almost always lost, almost always had the blame settle on him in affairs half of which he didn't even know about.

Remembering this, he put the bottle of wine a little more out of sight, tucked it under his arm, instead of dangling it, swinging it, with style, in the open air. And the mothers and fathers looked, he thought, a little less disapproving.

As soon as he was out of sight of the liquor store and had found a fairly quiet spot on the beach, almost under the boardwalk, he sat down and considered how to open his bottle of wine without the help of a corkscrew.

This he ended up doing by driving the cork into the bottle with his thumb. Parts of the cork powdered and mixed with the wine inside.

He held the bottle straight up and drank. He'd worked up such a thirst in his steady stride from the rope bridge to this place that he downed half its contents with the first chug. The aroma of wine, the bits of cork played in his mouth, in his nostrils, a little.

And immediately there was a change in the atmosphere, as if a transparent curtain had been dropped and unfurled and swayed now in the air, or as if someone had turned a celestial radio on, making ordinary sounds on a sunny day seem distended and haunting. The beach was crisp and glowed beneath his haunches—he was squatting, holding his bottle. A breeze seemed like the slightest silk scarf, sufficient to distract him. The blue of the sky was suffused with other tonic shifting colors, hidden just behind the blue, and the whole afternoon had become a game that was being played by someone careless and glad who didn't know what to do. Jim thought of the thing that *he* was doing at this very moment and that made him laugh, laugh out loud, it was such a victory, such a feat—and then he thought of what he and Mindy and the Bray twins had done two weeks ago in the Brays' cellar when their parents were away, and that aroused him, made him smile more quietly; it was a victory too.

He drank some more from his bottle, and then the scenes of himself with Mindy and the Brays and of himself where he was right now combined and were rushing with an echo through his head, the level beach dipping to an angle which made him lurch, stand to his feet suddenly, as if he were on a combination of merry-go-round and ferris wheel and trying to keep a hold on the two contradictory motions. He hadn't had anything to eat for three hours, and the wine was going straight to his head. The motion of the beach pulled him to the edge of the surf, to small waves which only unfolded, only plopped a little, rather than crashed or roared, but they still made a sound much bigger than anything his brain, in this condition, could fathom or find its bearings in, and, heedless of the shoes and socks he was wearing and his trousers still rolled down and the looks of consterna-tion which (this time, there was no question of his merely imagining it) he really was getting from respectable patrons of this stretch of shore, he staggered into water up over his knees and, for a long while, with the bottle still in hand, wandered there, around and around.

Then he dropped the bottle.

Its remaining contents vanished like a red cloud, instantly dispersed, into the clear green water. .

And perhaps it was the shock of this loss, in addition to the cool ocean breeze that was traveling just three feet above the waves, that sobered him up a little, with the gulls helping by making their cries pierce through. He waded back to where the land was, in a happy state of after-exhilaration, not even feeling like vomiting, but refreshed, fulfilled.

He walked down the beach at a slow pace now, eccentric certainly but no longer a threat, no longer harboring trouble—merely walking at a gait which suggested that he was, for the moment, free.

He was free and there was no one there to ask him any questions, no one there to put any slant on how to see this afternoon but himself. All his body was free, his arms and his legs and his head, his tongue still caught the taste of the wine, made him want to kiss the air (and this he did, letting his head fall back and all the muscles in his neck relax), but he had to find a bathroom now because the wine, in addition to going straight to his head and lingering on his tongue, had, one part of it anyway, gone straight to his bladder.

He drifted back up toward the boardwalk, trying to find a place, a men's room or restaurant or just a secluded spot (next to impossible to find on this crowded beach) where he could relieve himself. And, while he was searching, he came across someone who was doing what he had been trying to do—get drunk, only not with wine but vodka. This man was a little more serious about it than Jim, however. The contents of his bottle were almost gone.

The man had blond hair, but a dirty-blond not the bright sea-blond of the Bray twins, and not much of it either because it was crew-cut. Having no hair made his face look halfway like a dog's (a Labrador retriever's) and halfway like a bird's (an eagle's). It made it hard to tell how old he was, too. He might almost be ageless, transported to this moment from a distant epoch, another time. He looked stupid, but that might have been the effect of the drink. In addition to this he looked, to Jim's mind, ugly—ugly but interesting. Although he had no visible scars, there was something in him which looked as though he had been beaten, either physically or in some other more mysterious way, again and again; and this look of abuse was most evident in the suspicious glare he gave Jim upon noticing Jim was about to intrude. It was hard to tell how big he was because he was sitting down, but he looked like he was strong and, like Jim, he was wearing just a T-shirt and khaki trousers, only a different-colored khaki—he had apparently lost or hidden his shoes, because he was barefoot. Jim, still with his wet shoes and socks on, although his trousers legs weren't taking long to dry out in this sun, approached the stranger, asked him:

"What're you doing?"

He got no answer, only the same suspicious glare. The soft but pervasive aroma of vodka was all over and around this person and was the only thing which communicated itself to Jim as a reply.

Jim looked at the bottle.

"You on this beach then?"

This drew from the stranger a new glare that was

almost like a knife, but just when this glare seemed like it might do its greatest harm, with merely the contact of eyes, there was something in Jim that the stranger noticed which made him soften his manner just a little. He asked Jim:

"You in the scouts?"

"How can you tell?"

At this the stranger looked away—then looked back, but not at Jim. "Seen scouts goin' past all day. Seen scouts goin' past on this road in their goddamn station wagons, goddamn fathers driving 'em. There's a jamboree up on the Hook just there."

"I know," Jim said.

"*How* do you know?" the stranger asked.

Jim smiled.

The stranger smiled back. "You got away?"

Jim nodded yes.

"Well, good for you then!" then added, "I used to be a scout," in a tone which suggested that he might be infinitely older and wiser than that now. Without further ado, he filled Jim in on his story, while offering him a swig of vodka. "Been down in Florida—Florida's the pits, man, got lizards all over the goddamn road, cars squashing 'em, it's so fuckin' hot you can see their guts steamin', goddamn lizard guts stinkin' up the goddamn air and *they* just kicked *me* outta the goddamn *army*!" —this last bit of information coming out with a ferocity that hadn't quite been led up to. "Listen, the army's shit, man, you don't wanna take the shit they give you in the army. I was in goddamn basic training, and they give you this *shit*, I don't wanna take no orders from *no* one!"

He let Jim take this in and then asked him, "How old're you, man?"

"Eighteen."

"Then what the hell you doin' in the goddamn scouts, still?"

"Sixteen."

"I'm twenty. But they didn't kick me out because of no 'disciplinary' problem." He pronounced "disciplinary" as though every word with that many syllables deserved to be put in quotation marks as a sign of contempt. "They kicked *me* out because they—the goddamn doctor—says I was color-blind! That's right, *color-*blind, man! But *I* can tell colors! Mother-fuckin' sons of bitches!" and then, softer, "*I* can tell colors."

Jim first looked at the stranger's eyes to see if there might be some difference there, which there wasn't, and then asked, "See that cloud?"

The stranger said, "Yeah?"

"See the sky all around it?"

"Yeah."

"Okay, what color's the sky just there?"

"Blue, man, it's goddamn blue."

"Okay, what color is it when it gets down to the horizon there just touching the ocean?"

"It's blue, man, it's still goddamn blue."

Jim said, "I don't see why they say you're color-blind," and took a swig from the bottle, then handed it to the stranger, who, after taking a swig, said to him, "Blue wasn't the problem, man," and then, after a brief pause, resumed his story. "The army's shit, man. Got on the goddamn train and came back up here. You know how long the train takes?"

Jim looked at him, blank.

"Forty-eight goddamn hours from Orlando or near enough. Had a ticket to go all the way to goddamn New York, man, *New York*, but I got off in Trenton, I just had to get off that train, couldn't take it anymore, hitchhiked from Trenton to Long Branch, you know? There's no goddamn straight roads *anywhere* in this state, took me six lifts waitin' in the middle of goddamn nowhere to get here—walked all the fuckin' way up from Long Branch—and here I am!" he announced, then added, "Jesus!"

With two last swigs apiece, they finished the bottle. Vodka, Jim was discovering, was interesting. It didn't make you feel drunk the way Jim thought of as being "drunk." It didn't slur your speech or rob you of coordination—not at first anyway. Rather, it put a clear lusterless light right inside your brain; it made what was happening seem unreal and that was how it crept up and overcame inhibition. It made you ready to respond to what might happen as you might respond in a dream, with no terror of the consequences, as though you could always, if you wanted to, wake up. It made Jim feel bold with this fellow, it made him take the empty bottle from the stranger's hands and screw it mouth first into the sand; he was even going to ask the man his name, but he remembered another question, or request, that he wanted to put in first.

He said, "Hey, I gotta take a leak. You wanna keep a lookout and make sure no one's coming?"

The stranger said, "Sure."

Jim climbed a little under the boardwalk and had to kneel down while he peed. The underside of the boardwalk was dank, footsteps above made the timbers creak. The rising smell of urine, making a little stream which disappeared into the sand, accentuated the dankness. Jim turned back once to see what kind of lookout the stranger was keeping, but the stranger was looking straight at him rather than for possible intruders, and had a hand that was searching for something in the pocket of his army fatigues. When Jim climbed back out from under the boardwalk, the stranger took his hand out of his pocket, asked:

"You got any cigarettes?"

"Cigarettes? No, sorry."

"No cigarettes, huh?"

"Don't smoke."

"No cigarettes," he repeated, taking it in—then asked, "Well then, you got any J's?"

"Any what?"

"You know—dope."

At this, Jim could only shake his head no. And, in fact, this question, with the realms of possibility it opened, made him feel suddenly more drunk. The question was followed, in turn, by another.

"Listen, man, you know where we can find ourselves any *women* around here?"

"Any women?"

"Yeah, man, must be some women around here *somewhere*."

"There's one over there."

"Hey, cut the fuckin' shit, man. You know what I mean. I mean *women*."

"You mean, do I *know* any women around here?"

"Yeah, man, whatsa matter. You don't like women?"

"Hey, this is the first time I been around here. You'd know more where the women were than I do. You been around more."

To this, the stranger made no reply, but he seemed very pleased. Then, on a different tack, he started: "I'll tell you one thing, down in Orlando we had ourselves the best little cut of hash! Man, that stuff'd just blow you away. We had the Feds breathin' down our necks, but they weren't worried about the dope, man, they were lookin' for bombs. Someone'd said on the phone, 'Hey, man, these dudes over in this outfit here're building their own bombs, man, and nobody knows what the hell for.' I mean we offered him a little cut of hash, but he turned it down, he asked us if we got any bombs lyin' around the place here and we all said, 'No sir! All we got is this little bit of dope.' "

"What's it like in the army?"

"The army's shit, man, I tell you, I wouldn't ... I wouldn't be in ... I wouldn't be in there if you paid me a million dollars—and I was the best damn thing they had, too, and I'll tell you one thing. If this country ever goes to war again and gets invaded, it ain't gonna be the army's gonna save it, the army's full of shit, man, no chance the army's ever gonna get organized and angry enough to get its *laundry* done, the load of goddamn faggots! let alone fight a goddamn invasion. Listen, if it's a war, you may as well face it now—"

And, looking Jim straight in the eye, he put a finger to his throat and, in his imagination, cut it. He couldn't even speak for a while after.

It was Jim who finally prompted him:

"The army's no good then?" This was, after all, disturbing.

The question hit a nerve, the stranger got defensive: "I was the best goddamn thing they had and look what they do, they damn well kick me out! Color-blind!—shit! —I can tell a *nigger* when I see one."

"Where—where're you from?"

"Like I told you, Florida, Florida."

"No, I mean, where'd you grow up?"

"Oh, where'd I grow up? Right here, in Delaware, man."

"We're in New Jersey."

"Same fuckin' difference."

He gave Jim a look which indicated that he might possibly be getting angry, and his anger was unknown enough a quantity for Jim not to want to chance rousing it up anymore. He had no idea what might rouse or soothe the anger, however. He couldn't tell if his own company was wanted or despised, but either way he didn't feel capable of leaving just yet. There was nothing he could say, so he just sat, continuing to bury the bottle and looking up every now and then to study the stranger's face. The stranger didn't seem to notice or mind anyone studying his face. His mouth was drawn tight, tense, concentrating on something, no telling what. Something dim or bitter, hovering right in front of him, he found totally absorbing.

Then a smile broke out over the absorption.

Almost to himself, he said, "I did it. I was the one who did it."

"Did what?"

He turned to Jim. "Phoned the Feds, man, told 'em about those bombs."

"Was it true?"

"Shit, no!" He grinned. "I made it up—on purpose. You gotta keep those goddamn narks outta trouble somehow."

This was over Jim's head, it wasn't the kind of thing he had ever come across before, he certainly wasn't likely ever to come across it in Waynesboro, and he felt as though he were beginning to have had enough of it now. But there was more to come. The stranger sidled up closer, his breath was in Jim's face, Jim backed away just a little. The stranger said:

"Listen, I'm gonna tell you somethin'. You know the only ways we're gonna beat the Russians? There's two ways."

Jim sat, waiting to find out. The stranger began to move his hands as though drawing invisible objects in the air.

"Get these pigments, see, these black pigments you can't see through, and put 'em up in the sky, up in the clouds, make this huge black shadow all across Russia, bring 'em to their knees, kill all their crops, make it colder'n shit, then when they give in, you could send in the airplanes to clean it up, that's one way."

Jim waited, in disbelief, for the second way.

At the prospect of telling the second way, the stranger grew more animated than ever, his eyes jerked back and forth and around, and his head moved like a little boy's head, swiveling, brain-inspired. "But this other way's the best. Listen. All you gotta do is get this machine, see, put someone in it with some H-bombs, spin it backward and, you know—relativity, go as fast as light and, you know, you can go back in time, then all he's got to do is get out, plant bombs under Moscow, under the goddamn *Kremlin*, man, under *all* that shit over there, then get back in, come back in time and then the President can say, 'Hey, look what you got under the Kremlin there,' and they'll find this great mother-fuckin' H-bomb sittin' right under 'em and we got the button to blast it off, and then they *got* to give in."

Jim looked at him and said, "You think that's gonna do it, huh? You think that's the way to do it?"

The stranger looked at Jim, nervous now, his deepest innermost ingenious inspiration not having met with quite all the unqualified approval it so obviously deserved, so that, in defense, he aimed a blow as low as any blow, in his book, could be aimed. He said:

"Whatsa matter, you a goddamn fag?"

To which Jim, breaking through to common sense

now, but using the same language this stranger had been addressing him in all this time, replied, "You're crazy, man; you're crazy as shit. You're crazier than my father is."

The stranger was on his feet in an instant and coming at Jim before Jim even had a chance to get on his knees. And the blow which caught him when he was halfway up made him see black for a moment. He fell. There was a sharp pain in his back and it was the vodka bottle he'd fallen back on, but he didn't try to move off it; instead he let the stranger pin him right there. He felt amazingly calm. He closed his eyes. And it was a strange fight they were fighting. Apart from the pain of the initial blow on the side of Jim's head, which really had hurt, and the pain of being pinned down and having the weight of the stranger on top of him with the half-buried vodka bottle sticking into his ribs from underneath (he prayed it wouldn't break), the fight was painless. The stranger was either too drunk to hit hard and accurately or else he wasn't as angry as his face implied he was. At least, his interest wasn't so much in hurting Jim as in keeping him pinned. Strong hands kept Jim's shoulders pressed into the sand and legs scissored, interlocked with Jim's legs, till the place where they exerted most pressure began to ache under the weight. There was nothing Jim could do. He kept on top of the vodka bottle in spite of the pain it was causing him because it seemed to him entirely conceivable that, were the stranger to spy it and get an idea, that idea might easily be to break the neck of it off and let the sharp edge of it trail across Jim's throat. And he closed his eyes because he thought that the sooner he gave up, the sooner this might be over. He had never seen a crazy person at close hand before, but the look of working fury in the stranger's face (their eyes had met and that face repeated itself like a searing echo in his mind, after Jim closed his eyes) had let him know for sure that this one was beyond the pale.

The stranger's weight shifted slightly and Jim felt a hand go into his pocket and then a voice barked out, "You got any money?"

Then he opened his eyes and, just as the stranger's face contorted in a strange way, other faces appeared behind the stranger's, saying,

"What the hell's going on here?"

A voice behind Jim said, "Careful, he's got a knife."

The weight of the stranger lifted off him, leaving a floating emptiness behind.

Then Jim got a kick in the head in exactly the spot where the stranger had aimed his most effective initial blow. It dazed him.

One voice said, "Sorry."

Another said, "You all right?"

Jim let his eyes close again. He didn't understand the new voices. The sound of gulls crying was all he heard. And if that cry was one of melancholy, then it was equally one of freedom too, with no foothold anywhere, no resting place at all, no system, in vulnerable air with only chance comforts, unreliable, unsteady to a point where they might as well not be there. With his eyes closed, comfort seemed to be something he could choose to see or not to see, whichever he pleased. Comfort was a thing you invented. He opened his eyes. And what he saw, after he opened them, high, high above, was the gulls' wings like markers pointing in different directions, swirling and drifting toward the bottom of a light-filled sky, straight up. And what that made him wonder, with the ache of the two blows beginning really to throb and surround him now, was who was most free, most adrift, most likely to find comfort, himself or the stranger? And to what extent, even after this confrontation, were the two of them friends or enemies or, more to the point, part of the same thing still?

And where had the second blow, the kick in the head, come from?

The new faces staring at him (there were three of them, all lifeguards') had to be paid attention to now. They cut his contemplation short. He sat up slowly, looked around.

One voice repeated, "You all right?"

He answered: "Yeah . . . I think so."

A second one said to the first voice, "He's not wearing a badge," and then to Jim: "It's only three-fifty. That lets you use the beach for a week."

A third voice said "We could still get 'im. He went that way. I'd like to beat his fuckin' brains in."

Jim muttered: "Whose brains?"

The first voice, by far the most reasonable, said, "You'd never catch up with him now. And besides, even if you did, what could you do?"

"Three of us? We could plaster him, man!," which prompted Jim to look around to see if he could see his assailant. But the stranger was out of sight.

"Only three-fifty," the second voice informed him again, "and that lets you use the beach all week."

Jim said, "All week . . . ?" and then, "You mean you gotta *pay* to use this beach?"

"That's only fifty cents a day."

The first voice said, "For Christ's sakes, the guy's just been attacked with a knife!" and then asked Jim, "You sure you're all right?"

Jim asked, "He had a knife?"

"Didn't you see it?"

Jim said, "I've gotta get back somewhere, I've gotta go now." And he tried standing up—his legs were shaky.

"I'd love to get my hands on that bastard," the third voice said. But Jim couldn't understand why the guy should be so angry.

More people came.

Someone in a uniform, who looked neither like a policeman nor a lifeguard, was saying, " . . . disturbing the beach . . . but there won't be a fine this time."

Someone else said, "Maybe we'd better get your name."

Jim said, "I'm fine, I'm really okay, I've gotta get somewhere, though . . . I've gotta get going."

The afternoon sky was still bright, still fully illuminated, but there was something of darkness beginning to be hinted at, just out over the horizon, east, and he knew that at least two hours had passed since he'd taken off from the rope-bridge competition and that he'd better think about getting back to the campsite before supper, if he didn't want to be noticed as missing, which would, as usual, mean trouble.

He got up slowly and, standing on his feet, waited for the pain to shrink from a thing surrounding him, which he would have to struggle through, to an annoying but clearly defined ache on the side of his head.

The three lifeguards watched him.

Meeting each pair of eyes in turn, and ignoring the other people who had gathered, he took his leave and climbed up rickety wooden stairs to the boardwalk, then crossed the boardwalk and made his way to the edge of the highway, where he started on his hike back.

In an odd way, much unexpected to himself, after he'd walked the mile or two along the steady stream of traffic and had gotten to the turnoff into the park and up the Hook, he found himself almost as glad to be on the dirt road leading back to the jamboree as he'd been to find the highway and billboards a little earlier this afternoon. He felt satiated with alcohol and activity. And he felt expanded yet unrewarded, as though certain possibilities, in his contact with the stranger, had been sounded out and turned out not to be as fulfilling of a certain kind of promise as he'd thought they might be, so that his thoughts now went to the Bray twins and to a kind of companionship more easily accessible on ground which was more his own ground than the beach had been—his own ground, which the jamboree, no matter how offhand the contempt in which he held it, was. The sky was beautiful; the light seemed to settle through it layer by layer. Odd fragmented sounds from the more boisterous of his fellow scouts drifted out to him here. He was almost back, and the thought of having the walk behind him instead of ahead of him left him feeling relieved and a little light-headed. Everything seemed to happen in the right place at the right time, and he let himself be taken from one place to another, from right to left, from ocean to night. Already, on this dirt road, shadows, cast by the trees or by sounds his fellow scouts could make, were beginning to grow, to be long.

oger was the first to come out, and the high sound he made was the sound of panic, a sound which varies in its manifestations from person to person, but is unmistakable in its essence. In Roger's case the sounds were audible falsetto breaths, almost moans, breathed at rapid intervals—*ah! ah!*—like a heartbeat gone out of control. While he made these sounds, he ran in restricted circles behind the barbed wire which guarded the entrance to the bunker. He seemed almost to limp as he ran, almost to drag one leg as though it were no good anymore. And it was this and the terrifying sound he made that began to draw people's attention.

Scouts went past and, at the sight of Roger behind the barbed wire, stopped and looked. This was like something they might see on television—a performance inexplicable and, as far as they could see, unconnected with whatever conditions prevailed in their midst, but still hypnotic, arresting. A little crowd began to gather, but Roger didn't even notice them. It was as if even though he had his eyes opened he had them opened to something else, something these others couldn't see, and he had no consciousness of the scene he was creating.

One or two scoutmasters came along, and one of them said, "What's the matter with that boy?" And in more than one boy's head the thought flashed through that the blond boy behind the wires was like a dog that had come down with rabies and was in the middle of its fit and ought to be shot if someone could find a gun, but where this gun ought to come from nobody knew, so they all just watched to see what someone else would do next because surely there was someone in the crowd who would know and do exactly the right thing.

Nobody did anything, however, and it was only when Roger began staggering in exhaustion and fell first against the bunker entrance and then, by chance, against one of the fence stakes that held the wire up and fortunately not against the wire itself, which would have met him at face level, that anyone stirred out of this dream of observation and realized that the boy must be in some kind of trouble. And it was only after this, too, that any of their attention was brought to bear on the bunker entrance from which, they realized, Roger must have emerged, whereupon they began to imagine every unspeakable thing possible.

Having put these facts together, they began to take action. Roger had laid himself down, in an oddly gentle way, on the little patch of grass which the wire fenced in. Here he continued whimpering and moved his arms and legs some, but his movements got feebler and feebler as the moments passed.

An Explorer scout got out a fat pocket knife which, among other things, had a wire clipper in it. He began to clip the barbed strands carefully and methodically, pulling and twisting the wire back around itself, to leave a clear entrance. His movements were slow and clear and masterful. Several older boys went in then and surrounded Roger, who had his eyes shut now but was still breathing fast. They looked at his sleeve, found the *431*, and then they cautiously and gingerly examined him, but could find no injury, no obvious ailment. It was a mystery.

Still, they sent an envoy to the information tent with a message to be megaphoned all over the campgrounds, asking for a troop leader or an adult-in-charge from Troop 431 to come to the bunker marked with an orange flag, and two more scouts were dispatched to the top of the bunker, to the spot where Chris and the Bray twins had been two hours before, to take off their neckerchiefs, unfold them, and then wave them back and forth, to indicate the spot for all the jamboree to see.

A little group of figures, full of puzzlement and good intentions, now huddled around inside the barbed wire. For the moment, it seemed to them, after the initial excitement, there was nothing for it but to wait and see what happened, find out who this boy was in the hope that this might to some extent explain his behavior. They almost began to recede away from the event, to lose interest. The boy was sleeping now. His sleep wasn't anything which, after the first few minutes, could keep a hold on attention.

The sun was sinking in the sky but slowly, slowly, like a pearl sinking through tissues of gauze, each tissue resisting it for a moment, with a pungency, an interesting angle of light, and then giving way. The Explorer scout knelt by Roger Bray, and his face and, in fact, both their figures were dimmed a little, obscured by the heavy shadow which the bunker cast. Gulls floated, catching the light and taunting the shadow below—until everything stood deathly still.

It was at this point that Chris Castle emerged, calmly, silently, from the bunker entrance, with Billy, unconscious, slung over his shoulder, walking carefully because of Billy's leg, which was hanging at a most peculiar angle.

Again, as with Roger, for a full minute or two the crowd just watched, didn't know what to make of him. And Chris gazed just as steadily back at them, until his gaze turned from one of observation to one of supplication. "He's heavy. I don't know how to get him off of me."

Still no one moved.

"It's his leg," and immediately with his acknowledging that, the situation began to make more sense to them. "I'm not even sure I should've carried him."

The Explorer and an Eagle scout came to his aid. Chris knelt down and they helped ease Billy to the ground. Chris stood up again then, looked at Billy, and added, " . . . only no one would ever have found us in there," nodding toward the dark interior of the bunker.

Mr. Gough was the first of the troop leaders to arrive on the scene in response to the announcement. And what he said when he saw both the Bray twins lying on the ground and Chris Castle looking very peculiar, standing nearby, was "Jesus Christ!" It seemed to him that this was just what he had been expecting; that, it having been all smooth sailing up to this point in the afternoon, he was bound to have been presented with this accident to get in the way and become an obstacle, to throw off the rhythm and exasperate him.

The Explorer met him as he arrived and, indicating Billy, said, "This one's broken his leg, sir; we'll have to get an ambulance," and then, indicating Roger, said, "We can't figure out what the problem is with this one."

Then he turned away from Mr. Gough, found what he hoped was a responsible-looking boy, and dispatched him: "Go to the information booth and tell them we need an ambulance down here. We've got a broken leg."

Addressing Mr. Gough again, he asked, "They yours, sir?"

"No, they're not mine," he answered at first, and then, realizing the more likely purport of the question, added, "They're in my troop, yes, but they're not mine. Their father's on the campsite somewhere," with which it occurred to him to wonder where in the hell Jim was—nowhere in this crowd that he could see, quickly looking round—and what the hell *he* might have to do with this business. Then he stopped and took in the figure of Chris, who suddenly looked suspect to him.

The Explorer, noticing Mr. Gough's look at Chris, explained, "They were in the bunker, sir. This one," he pointed again at Roger, "came out first. Your boy over there carried out the one with the leg. A good job if you ask me." He indicated Chris.

A number of members of Troop 431 had, in the course of things, been drawn to the scene of the accident by now and they joined the crowd in watching—Danny McDaniels, the two youngest Wings, and, just arriving, Blue Berringer were all there—and they whispered, "Which one's got the broken leg, Roger or Billy?" "It's Billy." "How can you tell?" "You can always tell the difference between them—just how they act." "What's the matter with Roger?" "Look, it's bent. I wonder if it's sticking through the skin." "How did he break it?" "Is Roger asleep?" "Nobody knows." "*Chris* knows."

As if sensing the attention of the crowd upon him, Roger rose from his swoon, sat up, was dizzy; he looked around, smiled at all the faces ("He's awake!" someone said), all the vague faces of the crowd pressing in to see him and getting worryingly close to the wire. Then

Roger looked at Billy. Billy didn't move. He breathed softly, softly, but his lips were blue. His forehead looked very frail; his thin blond hair was brushed back from it as if Sleep had come and smoothed her hands all over it, sweeping it back, back, and leaving his mouth dropped open, too. It was something very deep he was in; Roger couldn't speak to him now. His arms were okay, but his leg—it was bent in a place where it had never been bent before. Roger followed the line of it, he followed the shape, and then he saw a dark spot on the green khaki trousers, he saw a shadow, he waited for a play of cloud in the sky to alter what he saw. But then he saw—did he see it?—the dark spot grow larger and, for an instant, seem to trickle. He waited for a play of cloud, but no cloud came, the dark spot didn't go away, the spot was what it was, *the spot was . . . the spot was . . .*

The high breaths started up all over again; Roger tried to back away from his brother's body as if fearing contagion. Someone said, "What's up with him *now*?" Someone else said, "Here we go again!" And the Eagle scout, grabbing hold of Roger (which made Roger cry out, falsetto moans which turned rapidly to sharp swiveling cries), happened to look where Roger looked, at Billy, and said, "Jesus Christ—he's bleeding."

Activity started up all over again.

A strange man stepped forward and said, "You hold on to *him*!" and the Eagle scout duly kept his hold on Roger. But the man said nothing more, he only watched.

The Explorer, meanwhile, knelt down by Billy, pulled out the fabulous pocket knife again, and chose, from among the myriad blades, a pair of scissors. Gently, he began to cut along the seam of Billy's trousers.

Mr. Gough pressed more forcefully into the little arena and asked: "Has anyone gone to get an ambulance? Has anyone gone to get a goddamn ambulance?"

"I did, I sent someone, sir." It was the Explorer who answered—without, however, looking up from his work.

This answer wasn't satisfactory to Mr. Gough, though. He scanned the crowd for a more reliable solution.

"You, Blue, go to the goddamn information tent and make sure they gotta goddamn ambulance."

Once again Blue took off, and nearly collided with Mr. Bray as he did. But Mr. Bray was going slowly; he hovered, as yet only on the edge of the crowd.

The Explorer said, still not looking up from his work, "Someone go get a blanket, not a heavy one—or a light sleeping bag'll do."

Danny McDaniels said, "Maybe he's dead."

Mr. Bray, now next to him, asked, "Who?"

Danny McDaniels, without thinking, said, "Billy," and then had a look of terrible alarm over his face.

Mr. Bray pushed forward with more urgency and boys began to cry, "Hey, watch it, now!" because they were having to strain actively against the pressure of the crowd in order not to be crushed against the wire. Mr. Bray tried to slip past, he said, "Please let me through, please let me through," not with any authority, but as if he were asking a favor of people much older than he, speaking not very clearly, so that he had difficulty.

Mr. Gough addressed the crowd again, looked for a face. "Someone go get a goddamn blanket. Someone— Jesus!—you, McDaniels, you gotta blanket?"

McDaniels's mother was much famed for providing him endlessly with more than the boy could ever possibly carry or pack into his pack without its falling apart.

"Yes, sir."

"Then go to the goddamn campsite and get it."

"Yes, sir."

McDaniels took off.

Then Mr. Gough and Mr. Bray were face to face.

Mr. Gough said, "Jesus!"

Mr. Bray looked sick; he pushed the rest of the way through, to where he could see.

Billy was lying on the ground; his lips were blue.

The Explorer scout had cut the trouser leg all the way up past the knee. There was some blood, but not too much. In the red and blue of where the bruise and wrong shape were, there was a cut and, poking out of it, just a sliver, a splinter, of white bone.

Mr. Bray got down on his knees, looked at Billy.

Roger, behind him, still held by the Eagle scout, said, "Billy's not dead. Billy's not dead."

Tension was at its height. The sound Mr. Bray made as he knelt by Billy and looked at Billy's leg was the mournful and desolate sound of his name, a sound like an animal's, a sound that had been stored up all along and had reference points quite other than the one at hand, a whole amalgam of accumulated griefs.

Mr. Gough again said, "Jesus!"

Chris Castle stood further back, awed, afraid of all the display involved in what was going on.

McDaniels came running back, clutching his blanket, slipping through the crowd to where Mr. Gough was, to whom he delivered it with a "Here you are, sir!" McDaniels was important for once, and not just someone who needed help from people all the time.

But no sooner had Mr. Gough grabbed the blanket and moved to spread it over Billy than McDaniels was forgotten.

They spread the blanket, they stood cautiously around in a circle, not moving, to protect the leg.

Someone would have liked to console Mr. Bray for the

mysterious grief he was feeling (knowing perfectly well that Billy would be okay), to put a hand on his shoulder at the very least and say, "It'll be all right." But they were all too shy or ashamed to.

Things went quiet for a moment now—the empty sound that was left after the sound that Mr. Bray had made seemed a kind of order that things had been restored to.

Mr. Gough, standing, part of the circle of people looking at Billy's leg, and thinking how this would ruin the smooth course of events he had envisaged for this weekend, now began to mumble and then say out loud, "Who's it? Who's it did this? Who's it's responsible?" and then, withdrawing from the circle and turning to where Chris Castle was standing, almost in the entrance to the bunker, demanded, "Who's it that's responsible?," more ready than he might appear to be to accept an answer indicating that the Brays were entirely responsible for their own mishaps, for his suspicion of Chris didn't run that deep.

But Chris instead asked, "Responsible for what, sir?"

"Whose goddamn idea was it to go inside that bunker?"

Chris made the mistake of saying nothing.

"What the hell dja do it for? Why in the hell didja do it?"

Chris's look seemed to imply that he thought Mr. Gough was asking the wrong kind of question or asking it in the wrong way. He made no answer, but only looked at his interrogator as though he couldn't understand what made Mr. Gough so angry, until Mr. Gough finally exploded,

"Whose bright idea was it to go in there, goddamnit?"

To which Chris replied, "Mine, sir."

This progress made, the question was put again:

"Why didja do it? Why the hell didja go in there?"

But now Chris began to smile—his peculiar smile, his smile that seemed to come from somewhere else, brought by something quiet and familiar. And here, indeed, came Mr. Davies, pushing through the crowd, just as Mr. Gough, not really certain what he was referring to now, whether to an inconsiderate interruption of the troop's scheduled weekend activities (because they ought to be gathering wood for supper fires now, rather than standing and looking at Billy Bray) or, more ominously, to some possible misdemeanor on Chris's or the Brays' part while inside the bunker, was asking in exasperation,

"For godsakes why didja do it?"

To which Chris now answered, "I heard a harp."

Ian came up to Mr. Gough and Chris, and then both men were asking Chris questions. They asked:

"Why the hell dja do it?"

"You heard a what?"

"I heard someone laughing," Chris said simply.

To which Mr. Gough, in disgust, once more said, "Jesus!" and was going to carry his inquiry further with "no goddamn nonsense," with "Mr. Davies or no goddamn Mr. Davies" (beyond any mere suspicion, he felt a distinct distaste for both Chris and his stepfather now), only he was met with a distraction.

For, drunk as he could be, in a kind of second wind of drunkenness, and physically invigorated by his walk from the highway, Mr. Gough's son, Jim, with a T-shirt but no shirt or scout neckerchief on, stumbled into their midst and broke directly into the magic circle. The circle turned, looked. Without thinking, they stood aside. Jim went straight to Billy. Billy's lips were blue. Jim put his lips to Billy's lips, began to breathe, came up for breath, tried to put his breath into Billy's breath.

Someone said, "Uh, you don't need to do that—he's breathing okay."

Jim appeared not to hear this.

"It's his *leg*," they went on to explain.

But, with the blanket in the way, this wasn't readily noticeable.

Jim tried to put his own breath into Billy's breath.

Mark Wing appeared on the edge of the crowd, having wandered from the direction of the holly forest.

And then Jim was being lifted off Billy and thrown to the ground by his father.

"Goddamnit!"

And it was a continuation of the beach fight when Jim threw his father a sidelong punch which sent Mr. Gough staggering. It was the same fight, only with Jim acting out what he wished he'd done then. Jim swung and bashed his father on the side of the head. Mr. Gough came back at him and pommeled his son with fists, blow after blow coming down on Jim's head and shoulders. And now Jim was kicking his knee up to get his father in the stomach, while his right fist delivered another blow on the side of his father's head. They were latched onto each other, fists flailing. It was an out-and-out fight being fought in much too close proximity to Billy's broken leg, which the others were trying to protect. Jim gave Mr. Gough another blow, on the same spot on the side of his fat head, which sent him reeling backward, and then Jim leaped on him, knocked him to the ground and made as if to finish him off with his fists. But three scouts, suddenly working together, acted to pull Jim off, drag him back, hold him to the ground. He didn't seriously resist them.

Everyone was stunned for a moment at what had just happened.

Mr. Bray had turned to look in horror. The Eagle scout had let go of Roger, and they both just watched.

Then Mr. Gough got up from the ground (he would have a black eye, everyone could tell—already it was swollen) and he went for Jim. The whole thing seemed not at all a surprise, but a very old, tired-out story which everyone had heard and suffered through a thousand times before. He started laying into Jim where the three scouts were holding him. And, while he beat him, he shouted, "Goddamn queer! Goddamn queer!" until Jim, infuriated, got a leg loose and delivered a kick that got Mr. Gough in the same spot on the side of his head as the first three powerful blows, and it knocked Mr. Gough right out. He lay back flat, arms spread, chin in the air, on the ground, as if, had this been winter, he were trying to make an angel in the snow.

Under his blanket, Billy came to and, turning his head and seeing Mr. Gough lying comatose on the ground, asked feebly, "What's going on?"

The Explorer scout, his attention back on his patient again after the exciting fight, said, "It's all right. You've broken your leg." He felt like a father when he said it.

And Roger, completely recovered, danced at Billy's side and sang, "We've broken something again! We've broken something again!," which made Billy smile before he dropped back off into indifference.

Mr. Davies, in a manner of speaking, took charge. He walked over, got the three scouts to let Jim Gough go, and then he took Jim aside and told him confusedly, "Take off out of here. I don't care where you go. Just take off for a while, and come back later."

Jim said, "But—"

Mr. Davies stopped him. "Just do as I say and take off—right?"

It was perhaps Mr. Davies's being foreign and so quiet-spoken that made the command effective. Jim took one last look at his father lying on the ground — and then slipped off through the crowd.

Ian turned to his stepson, said simply, "Chris." And Chris came up to within his range, but no further words passed between them.

Off in the distance, the first faint sound of a siren, traveling along the road at the bottom of the Hook, could be heard.

Mr. Bray turned and said to someone who had just arrived on the scene and didn't know what was going on, "It's all right. The ambulance is coming."

Jim Gough still hovered at the edge of the jamboree, undecided as to where to go . . . and then disappeared.

And now Mr. Gough began to come back to his senses. He tried to open his eyes, but already one of them was swollen shut. With the other eye, the good eye, and without having to move his head, which between pain and stiffness was locked into position, he could look up the side of the bunker to its top. And there he could see, along with the two scouts who were up there to flag down the ambulance when it came, Mr. Wing of all people, who was looking down at him, at all of them, having apparently chosen this high vantage point from which to see the exciting turns of event that had taken place in the past quarter of an hour. Mr. Wing appeared to be glorying in these events, to be smiling on them as though he were in a position to float himself down, to offer succor or to muse aloud upon nuptial bliss, from so high up, and make all the bits and pieces of discontent come whole and be satisfying in his half-believable way.

"Goddamn Wing up there on the goddamn bunker" was all Mr. Gough thought, however, before he let his good eye close in exhaustion and let himself sink not quite all the way to unconsciousness but to a waking dream in which the sound of voices and the approaching siren of the ambulance seemed much more physical and real and disturbing than Mr. Gough generally gave such sounds credit for being.

The ambulance arrived, followed by boys from all over the campground who had not already been attracted to the scene of the accident. It came to a halt and turned its siren off, although the eerie blue light stayed flashing. Attendants hopped out, leaving the engine running, opened the back doors, took out first one stretcher and then another to pick up their victims. The Explorer scout shouted to the crowd, "Clear a way! Clear a way!" and the boys all looked at the silent attendants, dressed in white, as though at rescuers in a movie they were watching. They said, "Look, that one's got a beard," but when the bearded attendant turned and gave them a smile, it was as if a spell had been broken. All that was left was the task of getting the bodies into the ambulance, and a darted smile, betraying something other than total absorption in one's mission, made the task seem mundane like any necessary chore to be done. With a bit of a struggle over Mr. Gough (whose size and weight were difficult to manipulate) and with extreme care over Billy, the attendants got their cargo into the back of the ambulance. Mr. Bray and Roger climbed into the back of the ambulance, too, unassisted, to accompany the victims to the hospital. The Eagle scout almost followed right in as well, to keep hold of Roger in the event of further hysterics, but he stopped himself in time and just stood there, while they closed the ambulance doors. Mr. Wing scampered down from the top of the bunker in time to catch, through the curtained windows of the vehicle, the sad profile of Mr. Bray sitting inside the ambulance and staring down, presumably at Billy, as though it were a tragedy.

The attendants, having accommodated all their passengers as best they could, prepared to leave. The siren was turned back on, a driver appeared behind the steering wheel, and the ambulance took off. All the way across the campground to where the dirt track cut from the jamboree field through the woods of holly to the main dirt road that covered the length of the Hook, a dozen or more boys followed, running as fast as they could and imitating the sound of the thing they were following with cries, high moans (several of them spreading their arms and being planes dropping bombs on foreign cities, shouting out over the din, "Air raid! Air raid!"), which echoed, echoed, echoed—until the sounds that they made, in the coming twilight, accompanying the siren, came detached . . . grew still . . . hovered . . . had no motion . . . were like red, luminous, mushrooming flowers.

The crowd at the scene of the accident dispersed, and when the members of Troop 431 (all but Jim Gough and the four who had been taken off in the ambulance) got back to their campsite, they found Mr. Berringer had started his fire already and was working on it so as to produce an all-surrounding bed of coals in which to cook his gingerbread-and-applesauce pudding.

Mr. Wing had to take charge now, and the first thing he did was take Chris Castle aside and question him as to what had happened. Chris told him simply that he and the twins had gone into the bunker and Billy had fallen three feet, maybe four feet, unexpectedly, in a place where there was nothing to stop him, and landed the wrong way on his leg. Mr. Wing said it had been the

Brays' idea to go into the bunker, hadn't it? Chris said that, no, it had been his own idea and that at first the twins hadn't wanted to go along with it. Mr. Wing said, "But Billy pushed his way ahead, no doubt." Chris said that, no, *he* had been leading the way, with Roger in back and Billy in the middle, because the twins were scared, it was creepy in there. Mr. Wing asked, then why hadn't Chris fallen in the hole instead? And Chris answered, a little confusingly, that it hadn't been a hole, it hadn't been *there*, it was somewhere else.

But when Mr. Wing asked Chris *what* had been somewhere else, Chris didn't answer.

Then, after a moment, Mr. Wing asked, "But didn't you boys take a flashlight with you?"

Chris answered that, yes, they had, but the batteries had run out. Mr. Wing then burst out again that he didn't see how, if Chris had been the one in front and Roger the one in back and Billy the one in the middle, it had been Billy who managed to have the accident. And Chris answered, as though an entirely different and more sensible question had been asked, that, yes, it had been Billy, and not himself or Roger, to whom this thing had happened. Whereupon Mr. Wing, giving his first hint of suspicion, asked, "Nobody pushed him, did they? That wouldn't be funny. Look what happened."

To which Chris replied, "We neither of us even knew that he fell."

So that it looked as though there would never be any clearing up of the mystery and, since it was time for supper, Chris and Mr. Wing took leave of each other; they both had chores to do. Chris went to find his patrol and get something to eat—he felt famished. Ian caught up with him first, however, and asked Chris what Mr. Wing had talked to him about. Chris said that Mr. Wing had asked him about what had happened in the bunker. Ian then struck a more serious and what he hoped was a more intimate note and said, "Listen, Chris, there wasn't any foul play in there, was there?" And Chris answered in the greatest surprise, but still staying calm, "No, sir!"

Nothing could have been better calculated to make Ian falter in his steps than to have Chris call him "sir" instead of by his name, but it appeared to have come about without any calculation whatsoever. What Mr. Davies couldn't know was that it was perhaps a simple and natural consequence of the boy's having felt himself to be under the pressure of interrogation—first the Brays', then Mr. Gough's and Mr. Wing's, and now Ian's—for the best part of the afternoon. And maybe Chris made it up to him by saying, "Let me go eat, Ian. I'm hungry."

Ian let him go, then went himself to eat with Mr. Wing and Mr. Berringer. These three men didn't have much to say to each other, but Mr. Wing made a comment that was very much to the point: that mealtimes were— and, he imagined, the rest of the jamboree would be—very much more relaxing with both Mr. Bray and Mr. Gough gone; that it was a terrible pity (and with this Mr. Wing broke into what was for him a surprisingly uncherubic smile) that Billy had to break a leg and Mr. Gough had to get beaten up by his own son in order for it to have come about, but wasn't it a great relief? Mr. Berringer and Mr. Davies openly concurred, but Mr. Davies privately felt that the greatest relief at the moment was that nobody thought to inquire about Jim Gough's absence, for which he was responsible. He had no clue as to the boy's whereabouts at all.

This was the last thing of this kind, Ian Davies again swore to himself, that he would ever undertake, whether it meant a full-scale confrontation with Laura or not. And indeed it was the last jamboree he ever attended, but no confrontation with Laura was necessary to make it so, for the very good reason that only two months later the Davieses were transferred to Japan for a year, not to Tokyo or Osaka or any other big city, but to a smaller place on the island of Shikoku where there wasn't a large enough American community for there to be a Boy Scout troop. Once again, Chris was able to come in on a school year two months late and so was more easily able to keep up a solitude which, in spite of the worry of his mother, he much preferred to any involvement with his contemporaries. To his way of thinking, he and his parents left Waynesboro just in time, just before the closed atmosphere of the place managed to overwhelm them.

On this particular night, however, neither Chris nor Ian knew anything of this imminent move—and they went through the ritual motions of the evening (all planned out by the council) with a simultaneously acute observation and difficult suspension of disbelief, a suspension which, difficult as it was, they continued to give all their effort to, for this, they thought, was in one way or another an element they were due to remain immersed in for some time to come and whose terms, therefore, they were going to have eventually to meet.

After supper (Mr. Berringer's applesauce-and-gingerbread pudding tasted delicious, even the uncooked parts of the gingerbread; all the meals prepared tasted good, infinitely better than food cooked at home), the fires were put out with sand and the members of Troop 431 gathered together to go in procession to the huge bonfire being prepared at the northern edge of the jamboree grounds. All the other troops of the council came there too, so that hundreds of boys from all over northwest New Jersey sat around a blazing fire which made a dome of light in the twilight sky. They sat around a fire on a spit of land, a half-crooked arm giving its challenge to the sea.

Explorer scouts got everyone seated on the ground (each troop brought its own blankets and ground sheets) and then a message began to spread around through the talking and whispering and horseplay, till it won its way and everyone was saying it:

"*Shhhhhh . . . ! Shhhhhh . . . !*"

The message rose and then subsided, leaving such silence that, in a moment when no one was breathing, they could hear the crack and pound of a wave falling against the sand on the ocean side of the holly forest. Then that too subsided, and what they heard next was the faint sound of bells.

Bells were in a rhythm, came from out of the holly forest, were accompanied by low yelps and the pounding of naked feet into silent sand. Then they were loud. Legs and arms were shaking them in the air and yelps turned into howls uttered from deep inside. It was an Indian dance and the boys dancing it (imitating it) were nearly naked, dressed in loincloths and feathers and trinkets, faces grotesquely painted and limbs pale in the firelight.

They danced and the dance had a meaning, which an Explorer tried to explain, shouting above the din:

"White Eagle flies like an arrow through the sun! The Jackal tries to swallow the moon!"

No end of adventures of a cosmic import were being represented on this night by white suburban boys in a place, a strange and eerie place in which one wouldn't want to be left alone in the dark, where the dance's originators (if the dance had any authenticity at all) might have danced it three or four hundred years ago, when everyone who would have been watching it would also have been shouting or joining in or on their feet and swaying at the very least, not sitting quietly and merely looking as these boys, row upon row of them, were.

There was, to be sure, a good deal of giggling and an occasional exclamation of surprise uttered from first one troop and then another, but these exclamations and gigglings were not quite in keeping with the spirit in which the dance was being offered.

For the members of Troop 431, the exclamation and moment of surprise came when they recognized two of the dancers as being, hitherto unmissed, from their own troop.

"Clay!"

"Blue—"

The Berringer boys were in there dancing and the dance seemed the natural setting for their remoteness. They were active in the dance, their feet and their arms went faster and more gracefully than anyone else's. And yet the expression on their faces was impersonal, as though they were gazing on something entirely soundless and arhythmic just in front of them.

If anything, seeing Clay and Blue in the dance made Troop 431 hush, after the initial recognition, and become more absorbed in the events going on, in patterns and rhythms being traced before their eyes, because Clay and Blue were, in a way, mysterious without being laughable; they were closer than anyone else in these boys' range of acquaintance to the quite genuine thing they were trying (almost in an effort *against* the Explorer's shouted explanations) to represent. And it was entirely in keeping that Mr. Berringer, though he looked directly at the dance without blinking an eye, seemed to be viewing it in a detached objective way, without any hint of pride or even recognition that it was his own sons who were taking part in it and representing the troop.

The dancing ended after only ten or fifteen minutes, and although the hundreds of boys hadn't gotten up and joined in, still the dancing had loosened them up and given them back an energy which had sagged slightly just after dinner. The settling of the night into complete darkness emancipated them too and left them free (along with the knowledge that they were far from any place where they could disturb anyone) to do what they wanted.

So, after announcements and ceremonies and awards of various kinds, which the scoutmasters and the older scouts liked to impose on them, were over, they sang for a while, and the songs they sang were fast songs; they sang:

Three! Six! Nine! The goose drank wine!

And they sang:

A sailor went to sea! sea! sea!
To see what he could see—see—see—

They sang at least half a dozen more songs like these with endless verses and choruses, the words to which, under any other circumstances, they could never have remembered. But they remembered them now.

And, when the songs had built up to a boisterous climax, the dancers came back and danced wildly, faster and faster, arms in the air, bodies whirling, doing mid-air somersaults, shouting too, louder and louder, until the performance reached its natural peak and the energy appeared to collapse, leaving a quieter, glowing kind of energy behind. They danced for a while longer, almost in slow motion, to a chant no one could understand. The huge bonfire which earlier on had lit them entirely and almost reached out and burnt them, collapsed now and its flames were quiet, like the flames of a small domestic hearth, as the logs turned to embers. The dancers wove in a figure eight, like a snake, around the fire, and then took off back toward the holly forest from which they had come, in a slow but heavy, pleasant rhythm.

Now there came slow songs. The night had taken all that it could take in the way of speed and sound, so they sang "Clementine" and "Red River Valley" and "Blowing in the Wind," one after the other, slower and slower. Then came the very last song, the slowest and simplest song of all, and it went:

> Kumbaya, my lord, kumbaya
> Kumbaya, my lord, kumbaya
> Kumbaya, my lord, kumbaya
> O, lord, kumbaya

And again it was something that they, white men, white men and boys, were using, as they used so much else, not knowing what it meant. Was it an Indian song, was it African, was it an old spiritual? They had no idea. But the youngest boys knew it was the saddest and most comforting song in the world. It made you want to sleep.

And that was what they all did next, as night settled down, pressed itself upon them.

A bugle started blowing "Taps" and a megaphoned voice (could it be a joke, the dry monotone way it broadcast something so different from what it usually broadcast?) started saying, "Sweet dreams—goodnight —sweet dreams, everybody—goodnight, goodnight . . . " They got to their feet, gathered and folded the blankets they'd been sitting or lying on, and then filed off slowly toward their campsites. Once in their tents, they pondered or talked for a while about the things which they thought were the saddest or biggest or most important or titillating things in the universe. And then night was going by and they were unconscious, dreaming in it . . . all but a few of them.

Jim Gough was in the dark on a beach not far off, drinking beer which he'd bought with money he'd stolen from a wallet in the men's tent. It was money from Mr. Davies's wallet, but Mr. Davies hadn't missed it yet.

Chris Castle lay awake in his tent, next to Mark Wing, staring up into the walls of the tent, which, as he stared, began to have a gray glow to them. He unzipped his sleeping bag, put on a sweater, and then stepped outside. The moon had risen over the jamboree and lit the field, imbued it with a dream kind of air, made it like a system of sleeping hands. It lit the tents silver and gray and made them look as if they were made of sheets of iron or some other more adamantine material, rather than pieces of canvas stretched taut.

The moon shone in a way that made you want to follow it, and the way to follow it was—up.

Chris moved across the field of tents and moonlight, found the path to the bunker. Once he heard something and turned around to see, but the light which the moon deposited gathered like a mirror and reflected back at him more light and silver, leaving an endless place where anything might hide. Chris decided to be indifferent to what might be hidden. He moved up the sides of the bunker, and when he got to the top he was out of breath.

He looked around and could see lights, it was like looking at a galaxy from its center sideways so that you couldn't see it turning on its wheel but only as a fine pointillistic smear of stars and light making a ring around you. The ring started close, on the shores of Raritan Bay, and it dropped almost invisible to where Raritan Bay reached back to Perth Amboy; then it came back again with the lights on Staten Island, which went along evenly until they led to the extravagant crystal lights marking out the spiderweb span of the Narrows bridge, which led, in turn, to the lights of Brooklyn, Coney Island, the Rockaways, lights which shone out and then swallowed themselves, shone and then were swallowed, perhaps because of shiftings in the air over the water between the place where they were lit and this place where they were visible.

Chris looked out at them. And then, when he retraced his steps to the path which led from the top of the bunker back down to the field, Mark Wing was standing there, looking at him, having followed him.

Mark Wing came closer, and it was clear he had something to say. Chris didn't encourage him, however, and merely stood in unhelpful silence until Mark decided he didn't need encouragement to go ahead and ask Chris, "You know how Jim Gough says we can beat the Russians?"

"How?"

Mark Wing looked out at the lights and, without looking at Chris, said, "Put a shadow on the air."

This, however, got no response and Mark didn't try to elicit one by hinting at the mysterious way in which this information might have been communicated to him. Instead, after a pause in which the unforthcomingness of a response was confirmed, he asked Chris, "Who did it? Who pushed him—you or Roger?"

This was a definite question, something everyone in the troop wanted to know so that, in accordance with the answer, they would know whether to make Chris a hero or not.

But once more there was no response. Chris was looking away from the top of the bunker, which left him heedless of Mark's questions and presence up here. This heedlessness almost made Mark relax. And almost relaxing made him feel inspired to utter his most secret wish, his most carefully guarded impulse, for that would surely draw some attention.

"It would be nice to start a fire up here . . . now."

But, after again getting no response, he didn't dare risk saying any more, but only looked where Chris looked.

What he saw was New York City and its surrounding area dispelling a surprising amount of the darkness in the sky much more efficiently than any little fire of Mark Wing's could ever hope to do, unless of course he were to set a whole city or forest on fire.

What Chris saw too was the lights of New York, but without feeling belittled or discouraged by them the way Mark did. Mark didn't say anything now. And up there, in the night breeze, Chris felt as though he were being fixed to the spot by something as strong as memory, or evasion, never to have this view from the bunker out of his sight or mind. Because it was, after all, the most interesting thing to think about or see. And, more than that, with its closeness and distance, it seemed exactly the kind of thing to which, increasingly, he most belonged.

A Note About the Author

Michael Upchurch was born in 1954 and
grew up and went to school in England,
Holland, and New Jersey. He received
his B.A. degree from the University of
Exeter (U.K.) in 1975. For the past
five years he has worked as a shipping and
receiving clerk in bookstores in New
York and in Raleigh, North Carolina.
Jamboree is his first novel.

A Note on the Type

The text of this book was set in a film
version of Century Schoolbook, a type
designed in 1894 by Linn Boyd Benton
(1844–1932). Benton cut Century
Schoolbook in response to
Theodore De Vinne's request for
an attractive, easy-to-read type face
to fit the narrow columns of his
Century Magazine. Early in the
nineteen hundreds Morris Fuller Benton
updated and improved Century in several
versions for his father's American Type
Founders Company. Century remains the
only American type face cut before 1910
still widely in use today.

The book was composed by Superior
Printing, Champaign, Illinois, and it was
printed and bound by The Maple Press
Company, York, Pennsylvania.

Book design by Margaret Wagner